ALSO BY RICHARD PAUL EVANS

The Mistletoe Collection

The Mistletoe Secret

The Mistletoe Promise

The Mistletoe Inn

The Walk Series

The Walk

Miles to Go

The Road to Grace

A Step of Faith

Walking on Water

The Broken Road

The Four Doors

A Winter Dream

Lost December

Promise Me

The Christmas List

Grace

The Gift

Finding Noel

The Sunflower

A Perfect Day

The Last Promise

The Christmas Box Miracle

The Carousel

The Looking Glass

The Locket
The Letter
Timepiece
The Christmas Box

For Children and Young Adults

The Dance
The Christmas Candle
The Spyglass
The Tower
The Light of Christmas
Michael Vey: The Prisoner of Cell 25
Michael Vey 2: Rise of the Elgen
Michael Vey 3: Battle of the Ampere
Michael Vey 4: Hunt for Jade Dragon
Michael Vey 5: Storm of Lightning
Michael Vey 6: Fall of Hades
Michael Vey 7: The Final Spark

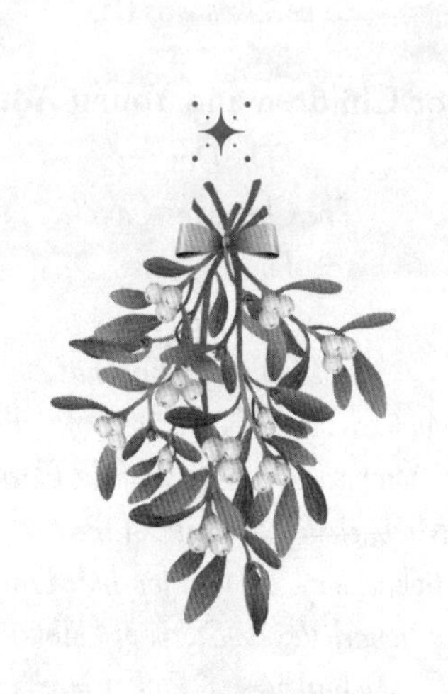

RICHARD PAUL EVANS

FROM THE NOEL COLLECTION

SIMON & SCHUSTER

NEW YORK LONDON TORONTO SYDNEY NEW DELHI

Simon & Schuster
1230 Avenue of the Americas
New York, NY 10020

First Simon & Schuster hardcover edition November 2017

Manufactured in the United States of America

1 3 5 7 9 10 8 6 4 2

Library of Congress Cataloging-in-Publication Data is available.

ISBN 978-1-5011-7203-8
ISBN 978-1-5011-7204-5 (ebook)

✦ *To Pam.* ✦

Wherever you are.

The Noel Diary

PROLOGUE

More than once, in the hazy dreamscape between slumber and consciousness, I've had a vision of a young woman with long black hair that glistens in the sun like obsidian. In this dream I am small next to her and she is holding me close to her breast, singing to me, looking lovingly into my face with her soft, almond-shaped eyes. It's always the same young woman I see. I don't know who she is or why she haunts the passages of my consciousness. I don't even know if she's real. But she feels real. And something inside of me longs for her. Whoever she is, she loves me. Or she did. And I love her.

This is the story of how I found that woman. And, on that journey, found love.

CHAPTER

One

Wednesday, December 7

CHICAGO

The reporter from *USA Today* walked into the Dunkin' Donuts looking harried and frazzled, which is to say, she looked pretty much like everyone else in downtown Chicago. My publicist had arranged the interview for two o'clock at the donut shop near Millennium Park. It was ten minutes past the hour.

She looked around the room until she spotted me, then hurried over. "Sorry I'm late, Mr. Churcher," she huffed, dropping her bag on the empty chair between us. She unpeeled the wool scarf that was wrapped around her neck and chin. Her cheeks and nose were red from the biting cold. "I should have taken the L. Finding parking in downtown Chicago is almost as hard as finding an honest politician in Chicago."

"No worries," I said. I looked her over. She looked

twenty-two or -three, twenty-five tops. They seemed younger every year. Or maybe I was just getting older. I sipped my coffee as she stripped off her outer winter shell.

"It's cold out there. I can see why they call it the Windy City."

"The name Windy City has nothing to do with the weather," I said. "The New York City editor of the *Sun* called it that because he thought the Chicagoans were braggarts."

"I didn't know that," she said.

"Would you like coffee?" I asked.

"No, thank you. I've wasted enough of your time already."

After grinding my way through more than five hundred press interviews I had learned to handle reporters with the same cautious approach one should take with stray dogs. They're probably safe but, for your own protection, assume that they'll bite. I also learned that saying "off the record" is tantamount to saying "Make sure your recorder's got batteries, baby, because this is the dirt you're looking for."

"How are you?" she said, looking more settled.

"Fine," I replied.

She pulled a hand recorder from her bag and set it on the table. "You don't mind if I record us, do you?"

They always asked this. I was always tempted to say no.

"No, you're good."

"Okay, then we'll get started." She pushed a button on

her recorder and a red light began to flash. "I'm interviewing bestselling author J. Churcher. This is for the Holiday Roundup edition." She looked at me. "Mr. Churcher. May I call you Jake?"

"Whatever you like."

"Jake, you have a new book out. It's still too new to have hit any lists, but I'm sure it will."

"I never take that for granted," I said. "But it's Wednesday. I'll find out about the list this afternoon."

"I'm sure you'll hit number one."

"Not likely, but we can hope."

"So what is this time of the year like for you?"

I took another drink of coffee, set down my cup, then gestured to the room. "It's just like this. A lot of travel. A lot of interviews. A lot of coffee. Sign a few books."

"You had a book signing last night in . . ."

"Naperville."

"Right. How did that go?"

"It went well."

"How many of your readers were there?"

"Five, six hundred. Kind of an average signing."

"How many cities was your tour?"

"I think twelve. New York, Boston, Cincinnati, Birmingham, Dallas . . . I don't remember the rest."

"You must be exhausted. When do you finish your tour?"

"This is my last stop. I fly home in four hours."

"Then you're headed back to Idaho?"

"Coeur d'Alene," I said, as if the city were a state unto itself. "I fly into Spokane."

"Home for the holidays. So what is Christmas like at the Churcher home?"

I hesitated. "You really want to know?"

"That's the focus of my story."

"Boring, mostly."

She laughed. "You spend it with family, friends . . ."

"No. I'm pretty much alone. I open presents from my agent and publisher, drink a couple spiked glasses of eggnog, then watch the football games I missed while I was on my book tour."

The reporter looked a little vexed. "Do you have any Christmas traditions?"

"Yeah. I just told you."

She looked a lot vexed. "What was Christmas like growing up? Any special memories that stand out?"

I exhaled slowly. "Define *special.*"

"Is there a Christmas you'll never forget?"

I grinned darkly. "Oh, yeah."

"Can you tell me about it?"

"Trust me, you don't want to hear it."

"Try me."

"All right. Christmas afternoon. I was seven years old; my mother came into my bedroom to find me sitting on the floor playing with all my Christmas toys. She was apoplectic, screaming at me for making such a big mess. She made me go to the kitchen and bring back a heavy wooden mixing spoon. Then she pulled down my pants and beat me with it. It was like a demon had control of her. She didn't stop until the spoon broke.

"Then she filled a suitcase with my clothes, dragged me outside to the street, and told me to go find someplace else to live. I stood there for nearly three hours, shivering in the cold. I wasn't sure what was supposed to happen or how it was supposed to work. I figured that mothers must do this all the time to children they didn't want anymore. I wondered if maybe someone would just come along and take me.

"Finally, after three hours, more than an hour after the sun had set, freezing and hungry, I walked back to the house and knocked on the door. It took her about five minutes to answer. She opened the door and just stood there, staring at me. Then she asked, 'What do you want?'

"I said, 'If I'm good, can I come back and live here?'

"Without a word she turned and walked back into the house. But she didn't tell me to leave or slam the door in my face, which I took as permission to come back inside. I went to my room and crawled beneath my bed and fell asleep."

I looked at her. "How's that for a Christmas memory?"

She looked back at me with horror. "Okay. I think I've got what I need." She hurriedly shoved her things back into her bag and put on her coat. "Thank you. This will come out a week or so before Christmas." She walked back out into the cold.

My publicist is going to hate me, I thought.

✦

If you've read any of my books, you know me better by my nom de plume, J. Churcher. My full name is Jacob Christian Churcher. It was only as a teenager that I realized how weird my name was and wondered if, to my parents, it was some kind of joke, like the twisted people who name their children Ima Hogg or Robin Graves.

Christian Churcher. JC Churcher. The name seems even more ironic since my parents never took me to a church.

You would think that a writer of love stories would be good at romance. Not so. At least not in my case. Maybe it's a classic example of those who can't do, teach (or at least write about it), but at the age of thirty-four, all I had to my name was an unbroken string of failed relationships. Still I kept trying.

They say that only a fool keeps doing the same thing and expects a different result, and maybe I am that fool, but I think it's more complex than that. I feel more like there's something hardwired inside me to sabotage my relationships.

Or maybe it's just like the song says, I'm looking for love in all the wrong places. When I was just beginning my writing career, a veteran author gave me this sage advice: "Never date a reader." I ignored this advice over and over, meeting women at book signings and starting relationships that lasted about as long as the flavor in chewing gum.

The problem is, women read my books and fall in love with the supermen I create. If they can't find that kind of man in real life (good luck with that), they sometimes supplant him with me. These are the women I had been dating. And eventually they discover that I'm just as broken and flawed as every other man. Or in my case, maybe even more so.

There's a reason for that. The breaking of my world began while I was still young. Two things happened. My older brother died and my parents divorced. I was four years old—almost too young to remember. August 4, 1986. That's the day Charles died. Everything changed after that. My mother changed after that.

My mother, Ruth, struggled with mental illness. Of course, I didn't know that when I was young. For years I just thought that life was supposed to be a daily nightmare of beatings and neglect. When you're raised in an asylum, crazy is normal. It wasn't until I was a teenager that the scales fell from my eyes and I began to see the experiences of my life for what they really were—messed up beyond belief.

My mother wasn't always cruel. There were times that she was sweet and sensitive. They were rare, but those were the times I held on to. As I got older, those moments became rarer. Most of the time she was just absent.

She often had migraines and spent a lot of time in bed, in a dark room, with the phone off the hook, hiding from light and the world. I became abnormally independent for my age. I got my own meals, got myself off to school, washed my clothes in the bathtub if they had something on them.

When my mother took to bed I would go into her dark room to see how she was. She would often ask me to scratch her back. She had a pencil that she had taped two toothpicks to and I would run it up and down her back or neck or arms. Sometimes for hours. It was the only thing I did that made me feel that she loved or needed me. Sometimes she would say sweet things as I scratched her, something I craved like oxygen.

The isolation I lived in wasn't just at home. I mostly kept to myself at school as well. I was a loner—still am. Maybe it was because I always felt different than other kids my age. I was sullen and serious. People said I thought too much. Also, I didn't have time to make friends because I had to keep my mother alive. She was suicidal and more than once she involved me in her plans to die. Once she handed me a carving knife and an electric knife sharpener and asked me to sharpen the blade so she could slit her wrists.

Another time, when I was a little older, I came home from school to find a garden hose coming out of the car's exhaust pipe and clamped into the back window of the car, the rest of the car's windows rolled up completely. My mother was unconscious. I dragged her out and laid her on the concrete floor of the garage. She had a terrible headache but suffered nothing else. I suffered for years.

By the time I was thirteen I was already bigger than my

mother and she stopped beating me. I figured that it was either because I no longer cried when she did it or because I could have beaten her up. Not that I would have. In spite of all the violence I'd experienced, I wasn't a violent person. I detested violence. I still do.

Memories of my father are hazy at best. Most of what I knew about him came from what my mother told me, that he didn't care about me. As much as I had learned to discount what my mother said, there was no denying that my father was missing in action and, from what I could tell, had made no effort to be a part of my life. In a way I was even angrier with him than with my mother. Why hadn't he been there? What was his excuse? If he cared, how could he have left me in such a place?

My last day at home was remarkably anticlimactic. I was sixteen. One night I came home from my job at Taco Time and everything I owned was on the front lawn. Even my pillow. The house door was locked. I never even talked to my mother to find out what I'd done wrong this time. It didn't matter. Something inside me clicked. I knew the time had come for me to leave.

I picked up a few of my things from the lawn, then walked back to Taco Time. There was a girl I worked with there named Carly who was always nice to me. She was a little older than me and had a car, a two-tone black-and-tan Chevy Citation. I told her that my mother had kicked me out, and she said I could stay at her place until I found something else.

Carly had also been kicked out of her über-religious

house when her parents caught her drinking alcohol, and now she lived with her sister and brother-in-law, Candace and Tyson. I helped her clean up at work, then went home with her wondering if they'd really let me stay. Her brother-in-law was a massive, tattooed Samoan man. Tyson terrified me. He was the biggest man I had ever seen.

But I had nothing to fear. Tyson was as kind as he appeared intimidating. He had an infectious smile and a laugh that rumbled like thunder when he was especially amused. He was also a devout Christian who, along with Candace, attended a nondenominational Christian church. He also went to a weekly early-morning Bible study with a group of men. When he found out that my mother had thrown me out, he was indignant. He told me that I could stay with them for as long as I needed to get back on my feet. Considering my age and situation, it was a remarkably generous offer.

Their home was small, less than seven hundred square feet on the main floor, with an unfinished basement and a dated Pepto-Bismol pink–walled bathroom. They didn't have another bed, but they had an extra queen-size mattress that they set on the floor in the basement. Just like that I had a new home.

Candace worked during the day as a legal secretary. Tyson worked in sales at an international phone equipment company, which granted him the luxury of being home by five thirty. Almost every night after dinner he'd sit down with me and ask what was up.

It was nice having male company. I wasn't used to it, but it was nice. I think he liked it too since Candace had little interest in most of the things he liked: rugby, hellfire-hot chicken wings, and Harley-Davidson motorcycles.

Even though I had left home, I continued to go to school. Actually, Tyson and Candace insisted on it, but I would have anyway. It wasn't the same school I'd been going to. Not even the same school district. I liked my new school, especially English and creative writing. Much of the reason was my teacher—a pretty, fresh-from-college woman named Janene Diamond. You hear about students having crushes on their teachers: that was me. I don't know if Ms. Diamond had any idea of what was happening in my home life, but I think that she sensed it. Or maybe she had a crush on me too (something I fantasized about). Whatever the reason for it, she took a special interest in me and encouraged me. She told me that I was writing at a college level and had what it took to be a professional writer. It was foreign to me to have someone so positive about something I did. I would often stay after school and help her grade papers.

Writing always came naturally to me. It was like speaking, but easier. Actually, a lot easier. I felt awkward standing in front of a crowd of people; it made words and ideas just bounce uselessly around in my head like microwave popcorn.

I believe that, for the most part, we don't succeed in spite of our hardships but precisely because of them. I think it was the drama of my life that gave me my stories and empathy. I had always created a lot of fantasy in my head as a survival technique. I spent a lot of time in different mental worlds to escape the real one and all its pain.

Without telling me, Ms. Diamond entered one of my papers into a district creative writing competition. I won first place. Tyson, Candace, and Carly all came to see me get the award. They called me up onstage and I was given a plaque, a leather notebook, and a Cross pen and pencil set. They were the nicest things I had ever owned. They were also, aside from a cupcake I'd won in a second-grade spelling bee, the only things I had ever won.

A year and three weeks after I'd moved in with them, Tyson announced that his employer was transferring him to Spokane, Washington, and we'd be moving in two months, just after I graduated from school. *We* would be moving. There was never any question over whether I would go with them or not, as they had assumed it. By that point, we were family.

Ironically, it was Carly who remained behind. She had finished her freshman year at the University of Utah and decided to stay in Salt Lake with her friends. The four of us boxed up the house, then Tyson, Candace, and I filled up a U-Haul trailer and the back of his truck with everything they owned, said a tearful good-bye to Carly, and drove the seven hundred miles from Salt Lake to Spokane—Tyson and Candace in their truck, me in the used Toyota Corolla I had bought six months earlier.

It might seem a little odd that I never told my mother that I was moving out of state, but I had no reason to believe that she cared to know. She had made no effort to find me since she'd kicked me out. I guessed there was just no point to it. It would be like telling a homeless guy on the street what channel your favorite TV show was on. Pointless.

Just a week after we had settled in Spokane, I got a job as a pizza delivery guy at Caruso's Sandwich & Pizza Co. I made good money in tips and they were pretty easy about feeding us, so that was a big benefit. I'd usually bring home whatever unclaimed pizzas were left at the end of my shift, which Tyson would happily demolish by himself for a midnight snack.

As summer came to an end, I enrolled at Gonzaga University in their creative writing program. I got a grant and good grades. I liked the college life. It wasn't the college life you see on TV, with wild, beer-chugging fraternity parties and such. Mine was a pretty solitary deal, but it worked for me. I spent a lot of time in the library and I wrote a dozen or so short stories, several of which were published in *The Reflection*, the school's journal of art and literature. I also picked up a little side money writing for the school newspaper, *The Bulletin*.

For the first time in my life I knew what I wanted to do with my life. I wanted to be a writer. My ultimate dream was to write books and be a published author. One of my professors was a published author. He wasn't exactly famous, but he had a following. I couldn't imagine that life could be any better than that.

I graduated with a BA in literature at the age of twenty-three. During my final year of school, I got an internship with a Spokane company—Deaconess Healthcare—writing their weekly newsletter and online articles. I was hired full-time upon my graduation.

Financially, things were going the best they ever had in my life. That's when I finally moved out of Tyson and Candace's place. They never asked me to leave—in fact, they seemed a little upset that I was leaving—but after all they had done for me, I just didn't ever want to put them in a situation where they had to ask. Also, after years of trying, Candace was finally pregnant, and I figured that it was time they had their own life.

I moved into a small basement apartment just a half mile from where they lived. We still had dinner together at least once a week. And every now and then I'd bring Tyson a midnight pizza.

I dated a few girls, but nothing took. There was one benefit to my loneliness. Without a significant other in my life, I had most of my nights free. A year after my graduation I started writing my first book, a twisted tale about a broken family. I never showed it to anyone. I started my second book at the age of twenty-six. It was better than my first, but still nothing to brag about. I began wondering if I really had what it took to be a novelist.

Fortunately, my passion was stronger than my doubt. A year later I wrote my first *real* novel. I call it my first "real" novel because it was my first book that I felt was decent enough to let someone else read. It was called *The Long Way Home*. It was a story about a young man trying to find his mother. It wouldn't take Freud to connect the dots about where I drew my inspiration from.

After finishing the book, I made a few copies and began sharing it with people at work. One of my colleagues, Beth, had a cousin, Laurie, who was the co-owner of a literary agency in New York. After reading my book, and without my knowing it, Beth sent the manuscript I'd given her to Laurie. It was like the time Ms. Diamond had entered my writing into the district competition without telling me.

I'll never forget the day Laurie called me. Our conversation went like this:

Laurie: Mr. Churcher, this is Laurie Lord of Sterling Lord Literistic. How are you?

Me: Who is this?

Laurie: My name is Laurie Lord. I'm with the Sterling Lord literary agency in New York. You wrote *The Long Way Home*?

Me: Yes.

Laurie: It's a really beautiful book, Jacob. May I call you Jacob?

Me: Yes. How did you get my book?

Laurie: My cousin Beth sent it to me. Apparently you work with her.

Me: Beth Chamberlain?

Laurie: Yes. She didn't tell you that she was sending me your book?

Me: No . . .

Laurie: Well, she did. And it's terrific. I'd like to take it to publishers. I currently represent thirty-two authors, seven of whom are international bestselling authors. I'd like to make you number eight. If you're interested, I'd love to fly out to Spokane to meet you.

Me: Uh . . . sure.

Three days later I met Laurie Lord, the woman to whom I would soon be professionally married. I signed a contract with her firm and she went to work, distributing the manuscript to big-name publishers. Six publishers wanted the book and it went to auction, selling for a quarter-million-dollar advance, which, needless to say, is a ridiculously high amount for the first book from an unknown author.

Within a month, the film rights were picked up by a

major production studio. It was an exciting time. It was also a major paradigm shift for me. My life suddenly seemed charmed.

Literary lightning struck. My book was both a commercial and literary success. The reviewer from the *New York Times* gave my book a stellar review. It also received a starred review in *Publishers Weekly*, and even the notoriously snarky reviewer at *Kirkus* gave it a nod.

My publisher contracted me for another three novels and I quit my job at Deaconess to write full time. My writing career was now what a million would-be writers dreamt of. Every now and then I'd wonder if my mother had read my book.

My next contract was for more than four million dollars. My life changed after that. A year earlier, Candace had given birth to an eleven-pound three-ounce baby boy. (Yikes.) That Christmas, to show my gratitude for all Tyson and Candace had done, I paid off their home and bought Tyson the Harley-Davidson Fat Boy he coveted. It was great to be giving to them for a change. Candace kissed me, while Tyson tried—unsuccessfully—to hide his tears.

"It's too much, man," he said.

I hugged him. "No, it's not. You saved my life."

I bought a home in Coeur d'Alene, a peaceful resort town a half hour east of Spokane. The home was on the lake and beautiful but, as in all wealthy neighborhoods, isolated. More and more I felt the loneliness.

Before she overdosed, Janis Joplin said, "Onstage I make

love to twenty-five thousand people; and then go home alone." More times than not, I felt that way. Not that I hadn't had offers. I remember the first city I flew into, I was met by a beautiful media escort. When she checked me into the hotel, the clerk behind the counter asked, "How many keys do you need?"

"Just one," she said. "He's alone." Then she turned to me. "Unless you'd like me to spend the night."

I pretended that I hadn't heard her. "One key is good," I said.

That was my life. A million fans. One key. And all the while, somewhere in my heart, was this woman who still haunted my dreams. A woman as elusive as an angel. I once tried to catch her in my writing but she eluded me even there. The story wouldn't come. I felt like I was fictionalizing a nonfiction story.

My life fell into a routine as predictable as a Tokyo subway car. I wrote a book a year and traveled around the country with a first-class ticket for one, meeting readers, signing books, and talking to reporters.

Then one day, almost three weeks before Christmas, I got a phone call that changed everything.

CHAPTER

December 7

I was in the car on the way to O'Hare when my agent, Laurie, called. "Churcher, you still in Chicago?"

"I'm on my way to the airport."

"Lucky you. I know how you love to fly. How did your interview go with *USA Today*?"

"No idea."

"That sounds ominous."

"It was."

"I have no idea what you're talking about, so I'm just going to let it go. So, I have the *Times* list."

"And?"

"Congratulations. You're number three."

"Who's one and two?"

Laurie groaned. "Man, you're hard to please. It's Christmas and you're running with the big dogs, Churcher. King, Sparks, Patterson, Roberts, and Grisham all have books out. Be happy with three. Your sales are up again; it's good. You're only competing against yourself."

"Tell that to the other authors."

"Good-bye," she said, not hiding her annoyance. "Have a good flight. And congratulations, whether you'll take it or not. Call me when you're in a better mood. Wait, wait," she suddenly said. "One more thing. I know you don't like to fly, but—"

"No, I *don't like* brussels sprouts. I *abhor* flying."

"Unfortunately you live on the wrong side of the country. We need to plan your trip to New York. Your publisher wants to know what day we're meeting."

"I don't know. I'll call back after my anxiety meds kick in. Bye."

"Ciao. Call me later."

I was about to set down my phone when it rang again. I looked at the caller ID. It was an unknown number with an 801 area code, something I remembered from my childhood. Utah. Even after all these years, just seeing the area code raised my blood pressure.

"Hello?"

"Is this Mr. Jacob Churcher?" It was an unfamiliar voice.

"Who is this?" I asked curtly.

"Mr. Churcher, my name is Brad Campbell. I'm an attorney at Strang and Copeland in Salt Lake City."

I groaned. "Who's suing me now?"

"No one that I'm aware of. I'm calling because I'm the executor of your mother's will."

It took me a moment to understand what he was saying. "My mother's will?"

"Yes, sir."

"My mother's dead?"

Now there was hesitation on his line. "I'm sorry. You didn't know?"

"Not until now."

"She passed two weeks ago. I'm really sorry, I assumed you knew."

"No. I didn't."

"Is there anything you want to know about her death?"

"Not especially. She had a funeral?"

"Yes."

"What was that like?"

"It was small."

"I'm not surprised," I said.

The lawyer cleared his throat. "Like I said, the reason I called is because I'm the executor of your mother's will and she left you everything. The house, some money, everything."

I didn't speak for a moment, and the man asked, "Are you still there?"

"Sorry. This is just . . . unexpected." Entirely unexpected. Like catching a taxi after a Broadway show on a rainy night unexpected. It's not that I didn't expect that she would die someday. Rather, I had so completely blocked her from my mind that having her suddenly barge back into my life was an interruption of my regularly scheduled programming and as jarring as an ice bucket challenge.

"Sir?"

I exhaled. "Sorry. I guess I'll probably need to come down to Salt Lake."

"It would be a good idea to see the property for yourself. You live in Idaho, correct?"

"Yes, Coeur d'Alene. I'll need a key to the house."

"My office isn't far from your mother's home. If you like, I can meet you and bring a few documents for you to sign. When are you planning on coming down?"

"I don't know yet. I'll call in the next week and let you know."

"All right. On a personal note, I have one more question."

"Yes?"

"You're not *the* Jacob Churcher? The author?"

"Yes."

"My wife's a big fan. Would you mind autographing a few books when I meet with you?"

"No problem."

"Thank you. It will mean the world to her. I look forward to meeting you."

I hung up the phone. *My mother was dead.* I had no idea how to process that. How was I supposed to feel? It's hard to admit it, but the very first thought that came to my head, unbidden, was this: *Ding Dong, the Witch is dead.* I know it makes me sound unsympathetic, if not outright crazy, but that's what I thought. Because even though I hadn't seen her for almost twenty years, the world suddenly felt safer.

✦

I called Laurie back. "I need to delay New York."

"What's up?"

"I need to go to Utah."

"*The* Utah?"

"Is there more than one Utah?"

"What's in Utah? Besides your mother and a head of bad memories."

"My mother died."

There was a long pause. "I'm sorry. How do you feel about that?"

"I'm not sure yet. I'm still letting it sink in."

"You're going for the funeral?"

"No. That was last week. She died two weeks ago. I need to go down to settle the estate."

"You sure that's a good idea?"

"Is what a good idea?"

"Going back. I hate the idea of you stirring those ashes. You never know what kind of fire it might ignite."

"I'm not planning on making any fires. Unless it's to burn the place down. I think I'll leave Friday morning."

"How long will you be there?"

"Not sure. Probably a few days. Maybe three."

"Flying?"

"Of course not."

"Of course not," she repeated. "That would be too quick and easy."

"I'll need my car."

"There are such things as rental cars."

"I like my car."

"I know you like your car. Do you need me to come out?"

"No. Thank you, but I'm okay."

She sighed. "All right. I'm sorry. I hope everything turns out all right."

"It will be fine. I'm just going back to settle a few things."

"That's what I'm afraid of."

CHAPTER

Three

December 9

COEUR D'ALENE, IDAHO

Laurie was right. As I prepared to leave for Utah, I wasn't sure if going home really was such a good idea. I wasn't even sure why, after so many years, I had so hastily offered to go back. It must have been something deeply subconscious because, in my conscious mind, I couldn't make sense of it. Then, after I committed, it just came together. I think that at least half the things I do are done out of inertia. Maybe that's true for everyone.

The last time I'd driven the route from Coeur d'Alene to Salt Lake was fifteen years ago coming the opposite direction with Tyson and Candace. That trip had taken us almost fourteen hours, but I was pretty sure I could do it in ten. For one thing, I had a bigger bladder than Candace did. And second, Tyson, pulling a U-Haul trailer in his old truck, pretty much did the speed limit the whole way. This time I drove a turbo Porsche Cayenne, which is basically a rocket disguised as an SUV. I can't remember the last time I'd driven the speed limit.

I made myself toast and coffee, then left my home at around nine in the morning. I drove southeast through Butte, Montana, down I-15 to Idaho Falls and Pocatello, across the barren, snow-covered landscape of the Utah border, then two more hours down to Salt Lake City, arriving a little after dark. I had made the trip in a little over ten hours, with only a lunch stop in Butte and a gas stop in Pocatello, Idaho.

The city was decorated for the holidays and the trees in front of the Grand America Hotel were strung with twinkling white and gold lights. The roads were clear of snow but there were three- to four-foot-high snowbanks on both sides of the streets. The city's skyline was larger than I remembered. Salt Lake had grown in my absence, and living in the smaller towns of Spokane and Coeur d'Alene had changed my perspective. The traffic was surprisingly heavy for that time of night. I guessed that there was a basketball game.

I avoided the hotel's massive porte cochere and uniformed valets by parking my car beneath the hotel. I rarely used valet parking. I hated asking for my car when I needed it.

The Grand America was every bit as grand as the name

boasted. The lobby was spacious, with marble floors and hung with brightly colored Murano glass chandeliers. The interior of the hotel was also dressed for the holidays with lush garlands, wreaths, and lights.

As soon as I got to my room I called the attorney. Campbell. He answered on the first ring. We agreed to meet the next morning at ten at my mother's house.

I ordered dinner—a beet and strawberry salad and some salmon—and lay back on the luxurious bed. The hotel was as opulent as anywhere I'd stayed in my travels. I'd come a long way since the last time I'd been in Salt Lake, when I slept on a mattress in an unfinished basement.

I still wasn't sure what it was that had brought me back. It wasn't the will. I didn't need or want anything from my mother. I suppose it was because there was still something dark inside me—something painful, like a glass sliver working its way deeper and deeper into my soul. Something I instinctively knew wouldn't just go away if I ignored it.

No matter the reason, something told me that I needed to go back.

I didn't sleep well. I had bizarre dreams. One of them was of my mother in a wedding dress. I came out dressed as the groom. I woke soaked in sweat and had to lay a towel down on my bed, since I wasn't about to call housekeeping to change my sheets at two in the morning.

CHAPTER

Four

December 10

I woke well after sunrise. I went down to the hotel's fitness center and worked out, then came back to my room, showered, and dressed. There was a text message on my phone from Laurie.

Good luck today. ☺

I'm going to need it, I thought.

I skipped breakfast and headed down to my car. Today my Porsche was less car than time machine, transporting me back to a place that existed more in memory than reality.

I had a plethora of feelings as I neared the old house. Driving down the old streets was like listening to an old vinyl record on a phonograph, with all the scratches and crackles, the surface noise as much a part of the music as the songs.

I hadn't been back to the house since I'd left Utah. In fact, I hadn't even been back to Utah. It's not that I hadn't had the opportunity, but I didn't claim it. The local papers, the *Deseret News* and its nemesis, the *Salt Lake Tribune*, had both written articles on me calling me out as a son of Utah—a title I had, at the time, no interest in claiming. I had refused interviews with both papers and turned down book signing requests and lucrative appearance and speaking fees simply because the venue was in Utah.

Now I was going back, without pay, media, or fanfare, quietly, like a thief in the night. Or perhaps a better simile would be like a veteran soldier making a solitary return to the battlefield where he was wounded. My own Utah Beach.

The whole neighborhood was in decline. And it didn't look like gentrification was in the immediate future. Nearly every home displayed an American flag or a crimson *U* for the University of Utah. Most of the yards were surrounded by chain-link fences or snow-laden hedges. In many of the driveways were cars old enough to be collectibles likely still in the possession of the original owner. I thought I recognized a few cars from my childhood.

As I neared the house, I could feel my anxiety rising. Everywhere I looked there were memories—mostly painful ones. Like the old run-down home with the plastic flamingos where a mean woman shouted at me almost every day as I walked to school because she was afraid I might walk on her lawn. Or the home two doors from it where I came across an old man illegally burning leaves. When he saw me, he blamed the fire on me and threatened to call the police. Maybe it was because it was a poor area, but it always seemed to me that there was a meanness to the neighborhood.

As I got closer to my childhood home, I could see the tall, twisting oak tree my brother, Charles, had been climbing when he died. I was watching my brother climb the tree when he accidentally grabbed on to a live power line and was electrocuted. I heard a loud *zap*, and then he fell to the ground a few yards from where I was standing. I was the only witness to the tragedy and ran home to get help. Even now I felt sick to see the tree.

Finally I came to the house. Like the rest of the neighborhood, it too was in decline. The house was a simple redbrick rambler with chipping white window frames and a single three-windowed gable on top. The roof was topped with more than a foot of snow and icicles draped from the rain gutters all the way across the roofline. On the south corner of the house was an icicle so large that it formed a column from the ground up, as in a cave when a stalactite meets a stalagmite.

Snow-covered concrete steps ascended to a small front

porch with a white, paneled front door behind an aluminum storm door.

Everything looked so much smaller than I remembered. I've heard that's the case when we return to the places of our youth. Maybe it's because we ourselves were so much smaller back then. Or maybe it's because our minds make things seem bigger than they really are, like the opposite of a car's rearview mirror.

The oversized mailbox was still there, coated in ice. As a small child, I always thought it was big enough to hold me. More than once, when I was six, I wondered what would happen if I put a stamp on myself and got inside. I suppose that's kind of telling in its own way.

The home's front yard was surrounded by overgrown hedges of pyracantha, their clusters of crimson berries brilliant against the snow.

There was a silver Mercedes-Benz coupe parked in front of the house with a couple inside. The man in the driver's seat glanced in his rearview mirror as I pulled up behind them. As I shut off my car, he got out of his and walked toward me. He was short with oily, neatly groomed hair. He wore a pink polo shirt, jeans, and loafers. I got out of my car to meet him.

"Mr. Churcher?" he said, reaching out his hand as he walked.

"You must be Brad Campbell," I said, shaking his hand.

"It's a pleasure meeting you," he said. He casually glanced at the house. "Does this bring back memories?"

I ignored the question. "Is that your wife in the car?"

"Yes," he said, looking slightly embarrassed. "Her name is Kathy. I'm sorry, she begged me to come. She was hoping to meet you."

"No problem. Tell her to come on out," I said.

Brad turned back to the car and waved. The door opened and his wife sprang from the passenger side like she was spring-loaded. She held a large canvas shopping bag that she lugged heavily at her side. She looked at me with an expression gravitating between fear and awe.

"Hi, Kathy," I said.

Kathy Campbell set her book bag on the frozen ground and reached out to me. "Mr. Churcher, you have no idea how excited I am to meet you."

Truth is, I had some idea. She was wearing mismatched athletic shoes. Or maybe that was a thing in Utah.

"Thank you," I said, taking her hands in mine. "I'm excited to meet you too."

"You're just saying that." She really looked like she might faint. "I'm sure you get sick of this, but would you mind signing a few of my books?"

"I'd be happy to."

"I brought a pen," she said. She handed me a felt-tip Sharpie pen, then stooped down and proceeded to lift the entire pile of books out of the bag. There were five in all, which she held in a column in front of her. "I have your other books too," she said. "I didn't want to burden you, so I just brought my favorites."

"Let's take them to the car," I said. I took the stack from her and set them on the trunk of the Mercedes and proceeded to sign them all.

After I'd finished she said, "Thank you so much. Can we have a picture together?"

"Of course," I said.

She lifted her phone. "Brad, come take our picture."

Brad looked embarrassed as he walked over. He took the phone and pointed it at us.

"Lift it higher," she said. "Always hold the camera higher. It hides the chin."

"I know, I know, honey." He snapped several pictures. "I got three of them."

Kathy stepped back. "Thank you so much, Mr. Churcher. My friends will be so jealous." She piled the books back into her bag and, with one last glance, returned to the car.

"I'm so sorry," Brad said, walking back up to me. "She's such a fan." He took a deep breath. "All righty, let's get this started." He reached into his front right pants pocket and brought out a metal ring with about a dozen keys on it. He went through the keys, detached one, and handed it to me. "Do you mind if I come in with you? I'd like to make sure things are in order."

"I don't mind." I turned back to the house and walked up the cracked, concrete walkway leading to the porch. "Careful, it's slick. I don't want you falling." I looked at him and smiled. "Actually, I don't want you suing me."

"I wouldn't," he said. "My wife would leave me if I did."

From the road, the brick house had appeared much the same as it was when I left it, though, like me, worn a bit and noticeably older. The inside, however, was a different story. I was shocked by what I saw.

The blinds were all drawn, but even in the dim lighting I could see that the room was crowded with junk. Actually, *crowded* isn't a strong enough adjective. It was overflowing. The room resembled a domestic landfill. Everywhere I looked there were piles of things, rising from the floor in dusty towers. I turned to Brad. "My mother was a hoarder?"

"That would definitely appear to be the case." He looked at me curiously. "She wasn't a hoarder when you lived here?"

"No. Almost the opposite." I found the light switch and turned it on. There were boxes stacked on boxes and newspapers everywhere, as well as bulging black plastic leaf bags. I couldn't tell what most of the things were, but some I could, such as open boxes of clothing, old paperback books—an entire pile dedicated to Harlequin romances—and stacks of VHS tapes. I lifted one. "VHS. Do you think she thought the medium was going to make a comeback?"

"This is probably why she never let me in," Brad said.

I looked around. "Doesn't look like she ever threw anything away." *Besides me*, I thought.

"Hoarding's an interesting behavior," he said.

I looked at him. "By 'interesting' do you mean bizarre?"

"It's a compulsion. All compulsions are bizarre."

"Look at this crap. This is its own kind of crazy."

"I had a lawsuit involving a hoarder once. A woman sued her own church over it. She had had knee replacement surgery, and while she was still in the hospital recovering, her Relief Society friends came in and cleaned her place. The woman kept everything. I mean, there was even a porcelain toilet in her front room.

"The women and other church volunteers filled two thirty-cubic-yard Dumpsters with her junk. After they finished, they steam-cleaned the carpets, even did some light painting.

"When the woman got home they were all there, excited to see the surprise on her face. She was surprised all right. She collapsed. She had a complete nervous breakdown and spent the next month in a psychiatric unit. She sued the church for three million dollars."

"What's a Relief Society?" I asked.

"It's a women's organization in the Mormon Church. The name sounds a little ironic in this case. It didn't bring the woman much relief."

"You represented the woman?"

"I represented the church."

"Did you win?"

He looked at me seriously. "I always win."

I walked farther into the mess. "It's cold. Think the gas company turned off the heat?"

"No. Utah law wouldn't allow it in the middle of winter." He pointed toward the near wall. "There's the thermostat."

I walked over to it. It was set at fifty-five degrees.

"Fifty-five," I said. "That would explain why it's cold." I turned the thermostat up to seventy-five. I could hear the heat kick on.

My mother had made a trail through the piles that wound its way through the house. Brad followed behind me as I found my way through the maze. It was like we were exploring an undiscovered landscape. We could have been carrying torches. Of course, if I'd had a torch, I would have been tempted to just toss it into the middle of the room and run.

"It smells terrible in here," I said. "Makes me think we should be wearing masks or something."

"We probably should. Hoarding creates all kinds of health risks. That's actually what I used to win the lawsuit against the hoarder woman. I argued that the woman had created a public biohazard as well as a fire hazard, and what the church people had done in cleaning it up was no different than shutting down a meth lab. She was endangering herself and the neighborhood."

"The jury bought it?"

"Yeah. Fortunately for us, she wasn't the most sympathetic individual. She kept calling the jury 'a bunch of idiots' and wanted the people who cleaned up her house to be put in prison for life."

I stepped farther into the room, to the edge of the living room, an ironic title, as nothing but mold was alive in this house. There were things I remembered from my youth. A quilted rendition of a Grandma Moses painting and a small resin replica of Rodin's *The Kiss*.

I remembered that there had once been a piano next to the fireplace. I honestly didn't know if it was still there, as all I could see was a mountain of boxes.

"I think there might be a piano under there," I said. "A Steinway. Her uncle left it to her."

"Steinway Model O, 1914. It's worth about forty grand."

I looked at him. "How did you know that?"

"It was in the will. It hasn't been played in twenty years. Maybe if you dig into the mountain you might find other treasures."

"Or I could just take a match to it."

He rested his hands on his hips. "You know, there are companies that specialize in hoarder cleanups. They come in and cart it all away. I could recommend one."

I kept looking through the piles. "Maybe. But not now. I want to go through it."

"Then perhaps I could recommend a Dumpster rental."

"That I could definitely use."

"Their number is 801-555-4589. I'll text it to you."

I looked at him quizzically. "Why would you have their number memorized?"

"They were called in to court as character witnesses in my hoarding case." He shrugged. "I remember numbers."

"Do you remember your wife is still sitting out in the car?"

"Yes, she's fine. She's rereading one of your books. There's not many authors she likes, so if there's nothing new, she just rereads yours. The funny thing is, she forgets how they end, so she enjoys it just as much as the first time. I swear the woman could plan her own surprise party."

I grinned. "I would appreciate the Dumpster."

"Let me call them for you. They owe me a favor. He glanced at his watch. "It's probably too late to have it delivered today and tomorrow's Sunday. I'll see if they can deliver it first thing Monday morning."

"Thank you," I said.

"You know, the house could be worse," he said.

"How could it be worse?"

"She could have had cats." He scratched his head, then said, "I'd better go. Call if you need anything."

"Do I need to sign any papers?"

"You will, but not yet. The will is still in probate. I filed it the day after your mother died; it will probably be another three or four weeks."

"So the house isn't mine yet," I said.

"No. But since there's no other caretaker, it's our firm's policy to contact the future owner so they can take care of the place before it's handed over. Before that we had a few homes burn down before we could deliver the title. What a legal mess that was."

"I see. Thank you."

"No, thank you. You made my wife's day, month,

and year." He grinned. "Heck, you made her life." He turned and knocked over a pile of boxes. "Sorry about that." He walked back out of the house, closing the front door behind him, leaving me alone in my mother's mess.

CHAPTER

I laid my coat over one of the cleaner piles, then began moving boxes away from the spot where I guessed the piano was. (Moving boxes around the living room was like one of those sliding tile puzzles where you slide one tile at a time to the open space and keep moving it around until you arrange a picture.) After I had moved an entire stack of boxes, my curiosity got the better of me and I opened the top one. It was filled with tattered *National Geographic* magazines.

I dug back into the mountain of junk. After moving the next pile, I uncovered the ebony leg of the piano bench. There were boxes on top of the bench as well as beneath it. I moved them back, then cleared the piano. My mother had set boxes and paper directly on the piano's keyboard. I uncovered it and pushed down on a key. Even with the lid shut and boxes piled on top of it, the sound of the piano resonated beautifully in the room.

I got up and walked into the kitchen. It was no cleaner than the living room and smelled worse. Ironically, the counters were covered mostly with bottles of cleaning solution, from what I could see, two or three of the same kinds, grease cutters, scrubbing pads, dishwashing soap.

There was a can of Lysol spray. I sprayed it, or at least tried to, but nothing came out. Apparently she had even kept empty cans. I opened the window a few inches to air out the room.

The small Formica-topped kitchen table was covered with stacks of plates and bowls as well as Tupperware containers and empty cottage cheese tubs. It was all baffling to me. She had lived alone and, to my knowledge, never had anyone over. Why would she need more than a few place settings?

Under the sink, I found an unopened box of plastic garbage bags. I took out a bag and began to fill it with everything that was unquestionably disposable, like a pile of Cool Whip container lids and a sizable collection of catsup and mustard packets from drive-in restaurants.

It took me about five hours to clean about half the kitchen. I had gathered the bags in a big pile outside the back door. I was covered with dust and grease.

The half of the kitchen I had cleaned revealed a long scratch on one of the cupboard drawers. That was my doing. I was only eight at the time. I had damaged the drawer when I tried to ride it down the stairs like a sled. Actually, I damaged more than the drawer: I also broke my arm. My mother no doubt would have beaten me had I not already been screaming in pain.

I felt a little like an archaeologist, digging through sedimentary layers, uncovering the past. But not someone else's past. My past. That's probably why I couldn't hire someone else to clean or just take a match to the place.

Maybe someday I would, at least figuratively, but only after I had found what I was looking for. I wasn't entirely sure what that was, but I was certain that there was something.

As I finished cleaning for the day, it was already dark outside and I realized that I hadn't eaten anything all day. There was food in the house, just nothing edible. I had opened the refrigerator and just as quickly shut it, the smell of curdled milk and mold-filled Tupperware containers was more than I could stomach.

I washed my hands and arms off in the sink, locked the back door, and, after taking one last look around, turned off the light and went out the front door. I stopped for sushi on the way back to my hotel. I hadn't even known what sushi was when I left Utah. I don't even know if there was a sushi restaurant back then.

That night I dreamt again of the young, dark-haired woman, only this time my dreams were especially lucid. These were the clearest dreams I had had of her so far. We were in my mom's kitchen. It was just the two of us and she was standing next to the sink. Something was wrong. She was bent over the sink throwing up. I was afraid that she was sick and might die. But then she looked back at me and smiled. "It's nothing," she said.

CHAPTER

December 11

I woke the next day to my phone ringing. The sun was streaming in through the windows. I rolled over to answer my phone. It was Laurie.

"Did I wake you?"

"No."

"Liar. How late were you up?"

"I don't know. I didn't sleep well."

"Sorry. I just called to see how things were going. Have you seen the house?"

"I saw it yesterday."

"How was it?"

"Interesting. There could be a book in this."

"I thought there might be."

"My mother was a hoarder."

"She was a mess, or she was a genuine hoarder, like on the reality show?"

"The latter. Every room was filled with junk."

"Was she a hoarder when you were little?"

"No. This is new to me."

"I read that hoarding can be a coping mechanism, triggered by a traumatic event. People hold on to things because it buffers them from the world and gives them a feeling of control."

"Trauma. Like my brother dying?"

"Yes, but you were with her after he died."

"More than ten years."

"So unless it was some crazy delayed response, something else must have happened." She sighed. "You're still sure that you don't want me to come out?"

"No. I've got this."

"All right. I'm around. I'm just cleaning the house this weekend."

"I'll send you some pictures of what real house cleaning looks like."

"I want to see those pictures," she said. "Good luck. Don't get trapped under anything. Oh, you're still at the Grand?"

"Yes."

"Try the eggs Benedict. It's out of this world."

"You've stayed here before?"

"I stay there every time I go to Utah. I have two authors there."

"Why haven't you ever told me?"

"Because it would be like telling John McCain you're planning a vacation to Vietnam."

"That was cold. Have a good day cleaning."

"You too. Talk to you tomorrow."

I hung up the phone, dialed room service, and ordered the eggs Benedict and an apple pastry with a glass of fresh orange juice. I was getting out of the shower when there was a knock on the door. I shrugged on one of the hotel's robes and opened the door. A woman stood next to a serving table covered in white linen.

"Good morning, Mr. Churcher," she said. "May I come in?"

"Please," I said, stepping back.

She pushed the table inside my room. "Where would you like to eat?"

"Over by the sofa," I said.

"How's your day so far?"

"Good," I said. "I just woke up."

She prepared the table for me, removing the cellophane from the top of the glass of orange juice and the metal lid from the eggs Benedict. I signed the check and she left the room.

Laurie was right. The dish was excellent. I finished eating, dressed, then headed out to face my mother's mess.

CHAPTER

Seven

It was a bright and clear morning, and the massive Wasatch mountains rose like great, landlocked icebergs. I had forgotten just how big the mountains were. And how ubiquitous. With the Wasatch Range in the east and the Oquirrh Mountains in the west, mountains surrounded the city like a fortress wall.

Salt Lake City is a religious city, and since it was the Sabbath there wasn't much traffic on the roads. I stopped at a Smith's Food King for bottled water, dishwashing gloves, a bucket, mop, cleaning rags, and several boxes of Lysol disinfectant. Then I drove through a Starbucks for a Venti caffè mocha before heading to the house.

The home was warm as I walked in, which was an improvement over yesterday, but the mess actually looked worse than I remembered—if that were even possible. I carried my coffee and my cleaning supplies to the kitchen and went to work. Inside one of the cupboards were boxes of Teenage Mutant Ninja Turtles cereal and Quisp, two cereals that were nearly as old as I was. I don't know what it is about old boxes of cereal, but frankly I felt nostalgic toward them. Maybe I had inherited some of my mother's hoarder instincts, but I couldn't throw them away. I finished wiping off the counter and was taking a sip of my coffee when I heard a voice.

"Hello."

I almost spit out my coffee as I spun around. An elderly woman stood in the kitchen entrance. She had whitish-gray hair and was slight of frame, though she wasn't stooped. Her eyes were clear and friendly.

"I'm sorry, I should have knocked, but honestly, after sixty years of just walking in, it didn't cross my mind." She looked around the kitchen with a slightly amused expression. "You're cleaning. This would have made your mother crazy." She turned back to me. "You're Jacob, aren't you?"

"Who are you?"

"You don't know?" she said. "I'm Elyse Foster. I live two houses down. I was your mother's friend."

Something about her claiming friendship with my mother bothered me. *My enemy's friend is my enemy?* What kind of a person would befriend my mother?

"I didn't know my mother had any friends."

"She didn't have many. How old are you now, Jacob? Thirty-four? Thirty-five?"

"Thirty-four," I said.

"Charles would have been thirty-eight."

The mention of my brother's name shocked me. "You knew my brother?"

"Honey, I knew both of you like you were my own." Her brow fell. "You really don't remember, do you?"

I shook my head. "No."

She stepped toward me. "I always said you'd be a lady-killer someday. You were such a beautiful boy. Big eyes. Big curly mop of hair. I was right. You're still beautiful."

I felt awkward with the compliment. "Thank you."

"You're writing books now."

I couldn't tell if it was a question or a statement. "Yes."

"I'm not surprised. You always had such an imagination." She looked around the kitchen. "It's always different after they leave, isn't it?"

"After who leaves?"

"The home's inhabitant. It's like the spirit leaves the house as well as the body." She looked at me with a sympathetic expression. "It must be difficult for you to be back after all these years."

"Very."

The moment fell into silence. After a minute I took a deep breath, then said, "Well, it's nice to meet you. I'll get back to work. I've got a lot to do."

She didn't move. "Don't be so dismissive of me, Jacob. You're not 'meeting' me. I'm a bigger part of your life than you know."

Her directness surprised me. I wasn't used to it. Once you become rich and famous, people don't talk to you that way. At least, not if they want something from you.

"And I know you have questions."

"How would you know that?"

"Because anyone in your situation would." Her voice suddenly lowered. "I may be your only witness."

I had no idea what to say to that so I didn't say anything.

She broke the silence. "How long will you be in town?"

"I don't know yet. A few days."

"Are you staying here?"

"No. I'm staying downtown at the Grand America."

"The Grand," she said. "Used to just be the Little America down there and Hotel Utah. Now there's a Grand America." She smiled. "I'll come back later. Give you a little time to digest things. Welcome home, Jacob. It's good to see you again. I was hoping you'd come home."

"This isn't my home."

"No," she said, frowning. "I suspect not. Good-bye." She turned and started to walk away, then stopped in the middle of the front room and turned back. "You know what they say about truth, Jacob."

"What's that?"

"It will set you free." She turned and walked out of the house, gently closing the door behind her.

I went back to work, Elyse's comment replaying in my mind. *My only witness?*

I took a break for lunch at around two, driving to a hamburger joint called Arctic Circle. I used to eat there when I was a boy. They had foot-long hot dogs and brown toppers—vanilla ice-cream cones dipped in chocolate. Arctic Circle is a Utah-based hamburger chain and the inventor of Utah "fry sauce," a surprisingly tasty mixture of catsup and mayonnaise. When I was young there were two unique Utah hamburger chains, Arctic Circle and Dee's Drive-ins, which no longer existed. When I moved to Spokane there had been an Arctic Circle, but I had never gone there. I don't know why. Maybe because it reminded me of Utah.

After lunch I went back to work, finishing the kitchen at around seven. I had collected more than a dozen garbage sacks with junk and dragged them outside the back door with the others.

When I had finished mopping the floor and disinfecting the countertops and appliances, I sat down at the table and looked around the kitchen. There had been life here once. I remembered Charles asking for Mickey Mouse pancakes and my mother making them with chocolate chip eyes. It was nothing more than a snapshot of a memory, but it was significant. My mother was smiling.

CHAPTER *Eight*

Monday

It was snowing the next morning. When I arrived back at the house, there was a large metal Dumpster in the driveway. Actually, it pretty much filled the driveway. I must have just missed the delivery because the truck's tire tracks were still fresh in the new snow.

I walked around to the back of the house, carried back thirteen garbage sacks, and threw them into the Dumpster. Then I unlocked the door and went back into the house.

The next room I decided to clean was my bedroom. It wasn't as bad as the kitchen. There were still the same four posters on the wall that I'd hung shortly before running away: a movie poster of *The Matrix*, one of Eminem, and two basketball posters, one of the Utah Jazz's Karl Malone, the other the famous Michael Jordan flying dunk poster.

I was surprised to see the posters still up. I guess I'd assumed that my mother would have torn them down along with any other reminder of me. But the room was mostly the way I remembered it, though back then it wasn't filled with boxes and strange junk like an old water cooler, a toy cotton candy machine, and about fifty empty plastic Coke bottles.

I had brought a Bluetooth speaker I could use to play music from my phone. Appropriately, I played my Red Hot Chili Peppers and Eminem, who had just hit it big about the time I left home.

Not only had my mother left my room exactly the way it was the last time I'd been there, but she had even made the bed and the drawers were filled with the clothes I had left on the front lawn the night I left home. It made no sense to me. Why would she have brought my things back into the house and put them away? Did she think I was coming back?

I was going through one of my drawers when the doorbell rang. I walked out and opened the front door. Brad Campbell stood on the porch. He was holding a tall Styrofoam cup that steamed in the winter air.

"Brad," I said. "Come in."

"Thank you," he replied, his breath freezing in front of him. He stepped inside. "I thought I'd drop by to see if they brought the Dumpster."

"It was here when I arrived. Your friends start early."

"They start work around five in the morning. There's less traffic to deal with." He handed me the cup. "I brought you a peppermint hot chocolate."

"Thank you."

He looked toward the kitchen. "Looks like you're making progress."

"It's coming along. Slowly. The kitchen took me all day yesterday."

He nodded. "It looks like a kitchen now." He put his hands in his pockets. "I'll let you get back to your cleaning. If you need anything, just call."

"I don't know what I'd need, but thanks."

"Don't mention it." He slightly nodded, then turned and walked out. I carried the bags from the room to the Dumpster, then came back inside, washed my hands, and drove again to Arctic Circle. I had their famous ranch burger with a raspberry shake, then went back to the house.

The hall outside my room was piled high with boxes. Since it was a main thoroughfare, it wasn't as cluttered as the other rooms, not that it really contained less junk, rather it was just slightly better organized.

I started going through the boxes. One of them contained all my schoolwork, from kindergarten to seventh grade. I was surprised that my mother had hung on to these things.

It took me about three hours to finish the hall. Almost all the boxes were filled with paper and documents of one kind or another. My mother had kept all her financial records and bills for the last fifteen years. The boxes were heavier than most of what I'd been carrying and, in spite of my daily appointment with an elliptical machine, I was a little winded after getting them all out to the Dumpster.

Next I started on the bathroom at the end of the hall. The bathroom was small and my mother had filled the tub with an eclectic pile of trash: unfinished knitting projects, two lampshades, and an old, rusted woman's bicycle with two flat tires and no seat. I had no idea what a bicycle was doing inside the bathtub, let alone the house, but I'd given up trying to make sense of the mess.

I was carrying the bicycle out of the bathroom when there was a knock at the door. I looked over to see the door open. Elyse Foster stepped in. She had snow on her hair and she was holding a cardboard box that looked too heavy for her to have carried through the snow.

"I couldn't imagine there would be anything to eat in the house, so I brought you some hot soup."

"Let me get that," I said, setting the bike down and taking the box from her. "Come in."

She stepped farther inside the room. "I made you tomato soup. You always liked tomato soup. You liked to crumble saltines in it."

"I still do," I said. "It embarrasses my agent when we're in a fancy New York restaurant. Old habits." She followed me into the kitchen and I set the box down.

"I put some crackers in there. Also some buttered rolls and a piece of chocolate cake."

"You didn't have to go to all that trouble."

"It was no trouble. Now sit down and eat. You haven't left the house since noon, you must be hungry."

I wondered how she knew I hadn't left the house since then. I got two bowls down from the cupboard. "There's enough here for two," I said.

"I've already eaten," she said. "I didn't want to force my company on you."

I came back to the table, unscrewed the lid from her thermos, and poured the soup into the bowl. "You're not forcing anything. Have a seat."

"Thank you." She sat down across from me and began unwrapping the crackers. She set them in front of me. "It's already looking much better in here. How is it going?"

"It's a lot of work."

"It ought to be. It took her more than fifteen years to compile it." She looked around and her expression grew more somber. "These walls hold a lot of pain."

"*These* walls hold a lot of pain," I said, setting my hand over my chest.

"I know. I'm sorry."

I looked at her. "You said something yesterday, about being my only witness."

"Yes?"

"What did you mean by that?"

"I meant that I'm the only one who knew you before the change."

"The *change*? You mean before I became famous?"

She shook her head. "No. Your mother's change. She

wasn't always the way you remember her. After Charles died, she changed."

"I was only four when he died."

"I know. I doubt you remember much of your mother before that."

I thought over what she'd said. "You said that you thought I would have questions."

"I think anyone in your situation would." Her face looked heavy with concern. "You don't know how I've worried about you over the years. Your mother was so sick. I'm so happy to see that you've done well in life."

I frowned. "I'm not doing as well as you think," I said. "That's why I write."

She nodded slowly. "I know. I've read your books."

I looked at her with surprise. "You have?"

"That's how I've kept track of you. I recognize many of the places and people you've drawn from. You've even put me in a few of your books, whether you know it or not."

I looked at her intensely. "How well did you know me?"

"You really don't remember," she said sadly.

"I'm sorry, I don't."

"Well, I shouldn't be too surprised. The mind blocks out painful times. I used to have those little Brach's chocolate stars. You would come over and ask for one of those almost every day."

"I remember those. That was you?"

"For years I took you whenever your mother had a migraine. When my nephew stayed with me, I would take you for days at a time. Anything I could do to get you out of that house."

Memories suddenly flooded in. There was a boy I would play with from time to time. He didn't live in my neighborhood, his aunt did. Sometimes we would go on adventures in the backyard, playing explorers or pirates; other times we would go to his aunt's house and play games. It was like we played alone, but together. But even he stopped coming around by the time I turned seven or eight.

"His name was Nick," I said.

"Then you remember him."

"You were his aunt."

She nodded. "He came to stay with me every summer until you were seven. His father was military and was transferred to Germany. You stopped playing at my house after that. That's probably why you don't remember."

"I always wondered why he stopped coming."

"Your mother became more secluded after that. I didn't see you as much."

"You knew my father . . ."

"Yes. I knew Scott well."

It was strange hearing him called by his name. "All I knew about my father is that he abandoned me."

Her brow fell and she shook her head. "No. That's not true. At least not completely."

"What do you mean, *completely*?"

"He left you, but it wasn't his choice. After your brother died, your mother stayed in her bedroom for nearly a year.

She withdrew from everyone. Your father felt guilty for your brother's death, and that was a pretty big club she had to beat him with."

"Why would he feel guilty?"

"From what I understand, he was supposed to be with him when it happened. Your mother blamed him for Charles's death. I think he was so grief-stricken, he blamed himself. She withdrew all love from him. After two years, he couldn't take it anymore. So they divorced."

She looked at me somberly. "You have to understand that your father wasn't doing well. He'd lost a son too. Only he carried the guilt with it. I'm not saying it's an excuse, but it's a reason."

"I never saw him again."

"Until just recently, neither had I. He never came back."

"Then he did abandon me."

She nodded sympathetically. "In a way."

Hearing her say that angered me. "*In a way*? He left and never came back."

She looked at me stoically. "If you want to see it that black and white, it's up to you. But life is more complicated than that. Motive matters. It wasn't what he wanted. And it wasn't his idea. Haven't you ever done something you thought was so bad that you lost faith in yourself?"

"I never had faith in myself to begin with."

"You must have had some faith in yourself." She looked down for a moment, then said, "Let me tell you something about blame. My brother took his own life thirty-six years ago.

"He was a very smart and successful obstetrician. He was delivering a baby when something went wrong. Both the baby and mother died. There was nothing he could do. Still, the woman's husband filed a malpractice lawsuit against him. It didn't matter that my brother was found innocent or that all his colleagues stood behind him." She looked into my eyes. "Do you know what group of people are most likely to commit suicide?"

I wasn't sure if it was a rhetorical question or she expected an answer. After a moment I ventured, "Teenage boys?"

"Doctors in malpractice lawsuits," she said. "It's because the very core of their identity is called into question. Whether they're guilty or not makes almost no difference. That's just the way we're wired.

"In a way, that was your father. It doesn't matter that your father was trying to help someone in need. It doesn't matter that your brother's death was an accident that could have happened even if he'd been home. He wasn't there and your brother died. That kind of thinking can ruin a person." She let out a long, slow breath. "I talk too much. And you haven't eaten your soup. It's probably cold by now."

"I'll heat it up in the microwave." I looked into the old woman's eyes. She looked tired. "Thank you for sharing."

"Considering the topic, I won't say it was a pleasure. But it is good to talk to you after all these years. I really have worried about you." She stood. "I'm so pleased that you became a good man."

"What makes you think I'm good?" I asked cynically.

She didn't answer. "I'll pick up my thermos later. Good night." She slowly made her way through the mess back to the door.

I put my bowl in the microwave and tried to start it but nothing happened. The microwave didn't work. I took my soup back out and ate it cool with broken crackers. As I sat there eating, I replayed our conversation. For the first time since I could remember, I wanted to see my father.

I finished the soup, then went back to the bathroom, finished cleaning up, and carried all the bags out to the Dumpster. It was snowing as I left the house—not much, just a few errant flakes here and there—but it looked pretty.

On the way to the hotel I stopped at a grocery store and picked up some more bottled water and trash bags, then drove back downtown. When I walked into my room, the message light on my phone was flashing. It was the front desk wanting to know if I was planning on extending my stay. I had already stayed longer than I had planned. I was starting to get the feeling that it might be a lot longer.

CHAPTER

Nine

December 13

I could tell something was different the moment I woke. Even in my room there was a peculiar stillness. I checked the clock. It was eight o'clock, but it was dark for the hour. I climbed out of bed and walked over to the window and parted the curtain. There was a blizzard outside. A complete whiteout.

From my eleventh-floor vantage point I could see Fifth South, the main thoroughfare to I-15. The street was invisible, completely covered with snow. Only a few intrepid drivers were on the road, crawling along at just five or ten miles per hour and still occasionally fishtailing. A block east I could see flashing police lights where two cars had crashed at the State Street intersection.

As I stood there my phone rang. It was Laurie.

"You didn't call," she said.

"When?"

"Sunday morning. You said you were going to call me tomorrow, aka, the day before yesterday."

"Sorry. I got busy. What's up?"

"How's the weather?"

"It's a blizzard."

"I saw that on my weather app. Did you finish cleaning?"

"No. It's going to take a while."

"How long is a while?"

"I don't know."

"Well, please find out—we've got work to do."

"I'll call you when I know."

She sighed. "All right. Be careful out there. Ciao."

I went back to the window and looked out. It's not often you see a city frozen. Then I got dressed and went down to the fitness center, where I worked out for several hours. Not surprisingly, the exercise room was slammed, everyone held prisoner by the weather.

By the time I got back to my room, the blizzard had lightened to a mild snowfall. Yellow snowplows with flashing orange lights looked like Tonka trucks below me. They were out in force, scraping the downtown streets, a mechanical salt spreader tossing salt behind them like rice at a wedding.

There were already significantly more cars on the road than there had been before. Salt Lakers are used to snow, and weather that would render a Floridian housebound barely warrants a sweater along the Wasatch Front. Utahans, like most people who live in cold climates, take a curious pride in that.

I took a shower and ordered room service. I should have ordered before my shower, because there was an hour wait for food, since no one was leaving the hotel to eat.

I turned on my laptop and pulled up the book I was currently working on, but couldn't get into it. I had written only a few hundred words when room service knocked on my door. The woman pushing the tray looked harried. "Busy?" I asked rhetorically.

"A bit more than usual," she said. "The blizzard's kept everyone inside."

I signed the bill, and she ran off.

It was almost noon when I finished breakfast. I looked out the window again and the snow had completely stopped. I knew that the freeway and downtown streets would be cleared before the suburbs, so there was no sense trying to go out to my mother's house just yet. I had another idea. I grabbed my coat and went down to the concierge counter in the hotel lobby.

"Could you call me a cab?"

The young woman behind the counter replied in a British accent. "You can catch one outside, sir. They queue near the front."

"Thank you." I walked out the gilded revolving door. A

young man in a hunter-green jacket and top hat nodded to me.

"May I help you, sir?"

"I'd like a cab."

"Yes, sir." He lifted a whistle and blew. An oxblood-red taxi pulled up. "There you go, sir," the young man said, opening the back door for me. I handed him a five-dollar bill and climbed in.

"Where to?" the driver asked.

"The Salt Lake cemetery," I replied.

The driver pulled out of the hotel's large circular driveway onto Second West. The traffic was still light as we wound our way through the downtown streets.

"That was some blizzard this morning," the driver said. "Shut us down for a while."

"I'm surprised at how quickly it stopped and everyone got back to business."

"That's the weather in Salt Lake, you know. It's the lake effect. You don't like it, wait a few minutes." He glanced back at me in his mirror. "Can't guarantee the roads will be clear at the cemetery."

"I'll take my chances."

About ten minutes later we pulled into the diagonally faced gates of the old cemetery. I could see that the roads had been freshly plowed.

"Whereabouts in the cemetery are we headed?" the driver asked. "It's a big cemetery. Here's some trivia for you: it's the largest city-operated cemetery in the country."

"Do you know where Lester Wire was buried?"

"Lester Wire?"

"The inventor of the traffic light."

"Hmm. No, but I can look it up." He pulled over to the side of the narrow, snow-banked road and consulted his smartphone. "Lester Farnsworth Wire. Inventor of the electric traffic light. It says here he picked red and green colors because it was Christmas and he had electric Christmas lights available." He set down his phone. "He's up on the northeast side." He pulled back onto the street. "And now I'll know who to cuss out when I hit three traffic lights in a row." He glanced back at me. "He a relative of yours?"

"No. My brother is buried near him."

"Gotcha."

We wound through the labyrinthine roads of the cemetery until we came to a vertical concrete monument and the driver stopped.

LESTER FARNSWORTH WIRE

SEPTEMBER 3, 1887–APRIL 14, 1958

INVENTOR

ELECTRIC TRAFFIC LIGHT

"There's your man. Or at least his grave."

"I'll just be a few minutes," I said. I climbed out of the

car. Even though we had only driven ten minutes from the hotel, we were higher in altitude and the temperature had dropped. I shivered as I pulled my coat tighter around me.

My brother was buried twenty steps to the right of a ten-foot obelisk with a cement ball on top. His headstone was level with the ground and subsequently buried in snow. I walked to the grave, felt the stone out with the tip of my shoe, then knelt down and cleared the snow from the marker's granite face.

I had been to this spot more times than I could remember. Enough that even after all these years I could find it covered in the snow. The tradition must have started early, as I had a vague memory of my father and mother lighting a sparkler and sticking it into the ground on Charles's birthday. After my parents divorced, my mother and I went alone. Three times a year. On Charles's birthday, on Christmas, and in August on the anniversary of his death.

But now it had been seventeen years. I stood up and looked down at the marker.

"You shouldn't have gone, Charles. Wherever you went, I hope you had a better time than I did."

I looked at the grave for a few minutes, then felt suddenly curious whether my mother's grave was next to his. I took a few steps through the snow, about five or six feet east of my brother's stone, until I felt another gravestone. I pushed the snow off with my foot, exposing the top of the marker.

RUTH CAROLE CHURCHER

REST IN PEACE

I sighed. Then I walked back to the taxi and climbed back in. "Back to the hotel," I said.

I must have looked different, because the driver didn't say a word the whole way back.

I didn't return to my room. Instead, I went from the cab down to the parking garage and got in my car. I waited a few minutes for it to warm up, then I drove out to my mother's house.

The south end of the Salt Lake Valley had gotten even more snow than downtown, and from what I could tell, my mother's neighborhood had been deluged with more than thirty inches. The entire place looked like an ice village, and cars looked more like igloos than automobiles.

A plow had been by, so the road was like a roofless tunnel with five-foot snowbanks towering on both sides. Those unfortunate souls who had left their cars parked in the street found the driver's side of their vehicles piled with snow up to their roofs.

I parked in front of my mother's house. I had to climb over a large snowbank to get into the yard.

It was already twilight when I arrived, and much of the home was obscured in shadow. As I neared the walkway I found footsteps leading up to the front door. They were recent enough to still be distinguishable: small, feminine-sized, with a small heel. I wondered if Elyse had tried to make her way over, but I decided that was unlikely. She would have seen that my car wasn't here. Besides, for an elderly woman, walking through this snow and ice was just begging for a broken hip. Still, I couldn't think of anyone else who would have come by in this weather.

I unlocked the front door and went inside. I flipped on the lights and walked over to the thermostat. I turned it up to seventy-five, turned on the music on my phone, and went to work on the space I'd dreaded most of all—the front room.

As I worked, I thought of Charles, the day he died, as well as all the times I went with my mother to the cemetery. I never knew how she would react. Sometimes she would fall to her knees and wail. Other times she would just stare angrily at the ground. Those were the times that frightened me the most. I never knew what Charles Day would bring.

I worked for about five hours, calling it quits a little after ten. I had managed to completely uncover the piano, which was my goal for the evening. I wiped off the bench with a damp cloth, took off my gloves, and sat down. I began to play. The piano was out of tune, but not horribly.

My mother had made me take piano lessons until I left the piano along with my home. With the exception of a few parties, I hadn't played for years. It was one of the things I had left behind, I think, because it didn't belong to me. Charles had wanted to play the piano. And a year after his death, the charge was given to me. I never wanted to learn to play and I hated every minute of practicing. Still, it was part of my past. It was part of me. And in spite of my resistance, I had been good once.

I began to play Simon and Garfunkel's "The Sounds of Silence." I remember one night my mother coming into the front room and sitting down while I played it. After I finished, she said softly, "Play it again."

It was the last song I learned, which is probably why I still remembered it. Or maybe it was because it was one of the saddest pieces of music ever written.

As I finished playing the song, tears were falling down my cheeks. For the first time since I'd heard the news of my mother's death, I felt loss. I pounded on the keys, then laid my head against the fallboard and wept. The thing is, I wasn't sure what I was feeling loss for. Maybe my mother. Maybe the loss of the mother I'd never had. Maybe my childhood. Maybe just everything.

As I sat there I remembered something. I got on the floor and slid my head under the seat. It was still there. Charles had written on it in black marker:

Charles Churchers piano

Five years later I had written beneath it:

You can have it

I stood back up, closed the lid on the piano, then locked up the house and drove back to the hotel.

CHAPTER

December 14

I woke the next morning around nine. On my way back to the hotel I had decided to keep the piano, so I looked on the Internet for a piano mover. The first two balked when I told them I wanted it delivered to Coeur d'Alene. The third was glad for the work.

I left the hotel early. The day was beautiful, the sky as blue as a Tahitian lagoon. I stopped at the Starbucks drive-through for a Venti coffee and blueberry scone, then drove to the house.

For the first time since I'd come to Salt Lake, the old neighborhood looked alive. People were out shoveling their walks or pushing snow blowers with great white arches spraying from their machines. One man was brushing snow off his car with a push broom.

The footprints I had seen on the walkway the day before were now iced over, preserved like winter fossils. I went into the house and went back to work in the front room. Now that I had exposed the carpet in places, I remembered it, an avocado-green shag that was outdated long before I was born. They say that if you wait long enough, everything comes back in style, but I think you might have to wait a few centuries for the avocado love affair to rekindle.

Several hours after I started cleaning, I came across boxes with Christmas ornaments and decorations that had been magical to me as a kid. The boxes still contained magic. Instead of pushing them out to the Dumpster, I opened them up, carefully unwrapping each treasure. One box contained old holiday records, a collection as eclectic as the season itself. Vince Guaraldi's *A Charlie Brown Christmas*, Kenny G's *Miracles*, Bing Crosby's *White Christmas*, the Carpenters' *Christmas Portrait*, *A Fresh Aire Christmas*, Nat King Cole's *The Christmas Song*, *The Perry Como Christmas Album*, Herb Alpert's *Christmas Album*.

I kept digging through the pile until I found what I was looking for—my mother's record player. It had been decades since I had used one. I had seen the old vinyl records coming back in vogue at the bookstores I signed in. I had even been tempted to buy a few albums; I just never got around to it.

I brushed the dust off the record player and plugged it into the wall. The tan, felt-covered turntable began spinning. I checked to make sure that the speed was set at 33 rpm, something I have no idea how I remembered, then I took the *Charlie Brown Christmas* album from the sleeve and put it on the player. Counting down the songs by the grooves in the record, I gently set the needle at track four, "Linus and Lucy." As the familiar strains of the song started, a smile crossed my face. Even in the worst of times, there had always been something healing about the music of Christmas.

Later that afternoon my phone rang. It was Laurie. I turned the record player down and answered.

"What's up?"

"You're number four," she said.

"I'm number four what?"

She paused. "You're kidding, right? Your book, dummy."

I had completely forgotten about the list. "Wow. It's already Wednesday."

"Yes, it's Wednesday, there's a new list, and you're fourth on it."

"Great," I said.

"What's going on?"

"I'm cleaning."

"I know you're cleaning, but what have you done with my author? You practically took my head off last week when I told you that you were three. It took me a half hour today to get up the courage to call you. I was prepared to talk you down from the ledge. I was going to tell you that the only reason you dropped a spot is that three more big books came out, including a Danielle Steele."

"No worries," I said.

"You're freaking me out." Pause. "Is that . . . Christmas music I hear playing?"

"Yes."

"So are you done out there?"

"Almost," I said.

"What does that mean?"

"*Almost* means very nearly, about, roughly . . ."

"I know what the word means. I want to know what it means in your specific circumstance."

"I only have the front room to finish, then I'm done. The piano movers come Friday to get the piano."

"You're keeping it."

"Yes," I said. "It's a Steinway."

"Do you even know anyone who plays the piano?"

"I play the piano."

"Another secret emerges from the past. So you meet the movers on Friday, then you fly home?"

"I drive home," I said.

She groaned. "I forgot you drove. Your publisher's driving me crazy about the next contract. I was going to try to talk you into flying to New York before going home. I guess that won't work."

"I can fly out from Spokane. I'll just need a few days to collect myself."

"Then I'll give them a definite *maybe* for next week," she said. "So back to you. How are you?"

"Good."

"Find anything interesting?"

"I found a lot of interesting things."

"Have you found what you're looking for?"

"It would help if I knew what I'm looking for. But no. Not really. Maybe there's nothing to find."

"All right," she said. "Don't forget me."

"Never. Ciao."

"Ciao."

I set my phone on the piano bench, then turned the Christmas music back up. I began listening through the Christmas albums. I was listening to Karen Carpenter belt out "The Christmas Song" ("Chestnuts roasting on an open fire . . .") when I heard a knock at the door. I turned down the music, walked over, and answered it.

I was expecting to see Elyse. Instead, it was a young woman. She looked about my age, maybe a few years younger. She was pretty. She had almond-shaped eyes and dark-umber hair that tumbled out beneath a wine-colored knit cap. She wore a long scarf and mittens that matched the cap. Something about her looked familiar.

"I'm sorry to bother you," she said in an uneasy voice. "But is this the Churcher residence?"

"Yes. What can I do for you?"

She looked at me anxiously. I couldn't tell if she was shivering from nerves or the cold. Actually, I had seen this kind of behavior before at book signings and I figured I had a fan. I wondered how she had found out I was there.

"Are you Jacob Churcher?"

Definitely a fan, I thought. "Yes."

"Ruth Carole Churcher was your mother?"

"Yes."

"Good," she said. "My name is Rachel Garner. I . . ." She hesitated. "I'm sorry, I'm a little flustered. I've been trying for so long to catch someone here, I really wasn't expecting anyone to answer."

I looked at her quizzically. "Who are you looking for?"

"I'm looking for my mother. Has your family lived in this house for thirty years?"

"More than thirty-five," I said. "I was born here."

She nodded. "Would you know if a young woman lived here about thirty years ago? She was pregnant?"

"A pregnant woman?" I said. "No."

She looked down, clearly upset. "Is it possible that you don't remember?"

"I would have been four, but it seems like the kind of thing I'd remember. Or know."

She looked even more upset. Actually, she looked heartbroken.

"Here, come inside," I said. "It's cold."

"Thank you."

She stepped inside the house, and I closed the door behind her. I could tell from her expression that the state of the room surprised her.

"I know, it's crazy in here," I said. "I didn't know that my mother was a hoarder. I'm just cleaning up the mess. I'd offer you a seat, but . . ." I gestured to the pile of boxes that hid the sofa. "But that's the seat."

"That's okay," she said. "I don't mind standing. Thank you for talking to me. I know it's a difficult time for you."

"Difficult?"

Her forehead furrowed. "I'm sorry, didn't your mother just pass away?"

"Yes. Of course," I said, feeling embarrassed that I wasn't experiencing the usual grief.

"I'm sorry," she said again.

"We weren't close."

"Then I'm sorry for that too," she said. She rubbed her hands together. "It's so cold in Salt Lake."

"You're not from around here?"

"No. I live in St. George. Are you from here?"

"I was born here, but I live in Coeur d'Alene."

She just looked at me sadly.

"May I take your coat?"

"Yes. Thank you."

I helped her off with her coat, then took it over to the piano bench, one of the few clean surfaces in the room. "Did you come by yesterday?" I asked, thinking of the footprint I'd seen in the snow.

She nodded. "In the afternoon. I thought I'd try again after that storm."

"How did you know my mother died?"

"A few weeks ago I saw the obituary in the newspaper, and I thought that maybe someone might be here and I could find some answers."

There was something about the way she said this that

stoked my interest. Maybe it was her vulnerability. Or maybe it was her beauty.

"I've got the kitchen cleaned up. We can sit in there." I led her there and pulled out a chair at the table, then sat down across from her. "It's Rachel?"

"Yes, Rachel."

"Why did you think your mother was here?"

"I was told that she might have been living here when I was born."

"Are you sure you have the right place?"

"I'm pretty sure. Scott and Ruth Churcher?"

"Those are my parents' names."

"I think my mother—my birth mother—lived with them. I was adopted as a baby, and a few years ago I decided to try to find out more about her, to try to find her. I went to the state but my adoption records were sealed. They sent a letter to her to see if she would be interested in meeting me, but she never even replied. I don't know if she's still alive or if she just doesn't want to have anything to do with me.

"Then, about four years ago, a friend introduced me to her new boyfriend. He worked in the state records department. I asked him if there was anything he could do to help me and he said he would look into it. He called me a few days later. He told me what I already knew, that the record was sealed. He said that he couldn't give me that information or else he could lose his job and face prosecution as well as a civil lawsuit. I figured that I was just out of luck. Then he told me something I didn't know. He said that my birth mother was only seventeen when she gave birth and wasn't married. He said that the record showed that my mother had come to live with a family with the last name Churcher. I think her family may have sent her away when they found out she was pregnant."

I looked at her curiously. "What year was that?"

"I was born in 1986."

I thought for a moment, then said, "I was only three or four years old. It's possible I could have forgotten. It was also a very traumatic time. It was the year my brother died."

"I'm sorry."

"Do you know your mother's name?"

She frowned. "No."

"No, of course you don't," I said. "My mother would have known. It's too bad you didn't come here before she died."

"Actually, I did. I came here at least a dozen times and rang the doorbell, but no one would ever answer. I could usually tell that someone was inside, but . . ." She sighed. "I even tracked down the phone number and called, but no one answered that either."

I wasn't surprised my mother hadn't answered the phone. She rarely did when I lived with her, and it appeared that she had become even more of a recluse in her last days.

"When I came across the obituary for your mother, I figured that if there was family, they might be here."

"And you might find someone who knew about your mother."

She nodded. "I was hoping."

I took a deep breath. "I'm sorry. I wish I could help you."

Her eyes welled up with tears. She looked down for moment, then said, "Do you have any siblings or relatives who might know anything?"

"I only had my brother. And my mother was an only child."

"What about your father?"

"That's another dead end. I don't have any contact with him. I don't even know where he lives."

She wiped a tear from her cheek. "I'm sorry." I could tell she was becoming more emotional, as her eyes welled still more. Suddenly she started to stand. "I've wasted enough of your time. I'm sorry to bother you."

"Wait," I said, a thought occurring to me. "There's an elderly woman who came by to visit. She was my mother's best friend. She's lived in the neighborhood longer than I've been alive. She ought to know. She just lives a couple houses from here."

Her face lit up. "Could you ask her?"

"We can go ask her right now."

"Thank you."

I helped her back on with her coat, then got my own and we walked out.

"Watch your step," I said. "It's pretty icy."

"I know. I fell trying to get over that snowbank. I'm glad no one was watching."

We walked down the drive and I helped her over the bank, then straddled it myself to get over. We crossed the street and walked up to Elyse's front door. I rang the doorbell. I could hear a chime inside, but no one came. Then Rachel knocked with her gloved hand.

I looked at her and laughed. "That was about as loud as a kitten falling onto a pillow."

"Nice use of simile," she said.

"It's my job. I'm a writer." I rang the doorbell again, then pounded on the door. Nothing.

"What kind of writer?" she asked.

"Books. Mostly."

"That's cool," she said. "Can you make a living doing that?"

I smiled. "Some do. I get by."

"I admire people who throw caution to the wind to pursue their dreams."

"Throwing it every day," I said. It pleased me that she didn't know who I was.

"Look," she said, returning to the matter at hand. "There's just one set of tire tracks in the driveway. She must have left."

"Good deduction," I said. "Let's go back."

We walked back across the street. Once we were inside the house, I took off my coat and said, "I'll tell you what. Give me your phone number and I'll call you once I talk to her."

"Thank you. Do you have something to write on?"

"I'll put it in my phone." I input her number, then

said, "You mentioned that you wouldn't be up here that long . . ."

She frowned. "No. I've got to get back to St. George by Saturday."

"Work?"

"No. I'm kind of between jobs."

"What do you do?"

"I *was* a dental assistant, but my boss retired. I don't think I'll have much trouble finding work, but I thought, as long as I'm free, I'd look again. But it's bugging my fiancé. He thinks I'm crazy."

Hearing that she had a fiancé bothered me. "Your fiancé?"

"Yes. Brandon. We finally set a wedding date for next April, so he's nervous that I'm not working enough and saving money right now."

I just nodded.

"The truth is, he thinks this whole thing is a waste of time."

"What 'whole thing'?"

"Looking for my mother. He says, 'So you find her, then what? It's not like you can change anything. What are you even going to say? Hi, I'm the baby you didn't want.' He's just practical that way."

Practical wasn't the word that came to mind. "What would you say to her?"

"I don't know. I think in the moment I'll know. Her eyes met mine, and I couldn't believe how beautiful she looked. "That probably sounds dumb to you."

"No," I said. "I understand why you need to find her. It's the same reason millions of people do their genealogy. They're looking for clues to who they are. It's the same reason I'm cleaning my mother's house."

Her expression relaxed. "Thank you for understanding. I was beginning to feel like I was crazy."

"I'm sorry your fiancé makes you feel that way. It's not right." I breathed out heavily. "Well, I better get back to cleaning."

Her eyes panned the room. "Do you want some help?"

I looked at her with surprise. "You're offering to help me clean this dump?"

She shrugged. "Why not? I have to go right now, but I have nothing tomorrow. And when your neighbor gets home, we can talk to her."

I wasn't sure why she was offering, but I liked the idea of having her around.

"I'd be a fool to pass that up."

She smiled. "Tomorrow it is. What time do we start?"

"I usually get here in the morning around ten."

"I'll be here," she said. She smiled at me. "I'd better go." I followed her to the door and opened it for her. She looked into my eyes. She looked vulnerable again. "Thank you for caring. I don't know why you do, but thank you."

"It's my pleasure. I look forward to seeing you tomorrow."

"Me too. Bye."

She carefully walked down the snowy walkway, awkwardly climbing over the snowbank. I watched from the doorway as she got to her car. Before climbing in, she looked back once more. She smiled and waved to me. I waved back. There was something about her that was different from any woman I'd ever met. Something about her felt like home.

CHAPTER

Eleven

The things my mother kept were inexplicable. Old dishes, pots, unfinished crocheting projects, stacks of every magazine you could think of, paperback books (none of mine), eight-tracks, a porcelain hula dancer. The place was like a flea market on crack.

I learned things about my mother that I hadn't known. For one thing, she had a Troll Doll collection unlike anything I had ever seen. It took up three boxes. The trolls were in mint condition and I didn't feel good about throwing them away, so I stacked them up in the hallway to give to charity.

I hadn't eaten lunch and was about to go out to get dinner when there was again a knock at the door. This time it was Elyse. Again she had brought food. "I brought you some dinner," she said.

"Come in," I said, stepping back.

She walked directly to the kitchen and set the food on the table. "I just came from a funeral. When you get to my age, it's pretty much the main social activity. I helped make supper for the family. The usual funeral fare: fried chicken, funeral potatoes, green Jell-O with grated carrots, strawberry salad, and potato rolls. The rolls just came from the store, so they're nothing to write home about."

"Funeral potatoes?" I asked.

"I know, it's a ghastly name," she said. "Sounds like you're eating something from a casket. But they are delicious."

"Now I'm really intrigued. What are they?"

"Nothing fancy. It's a Mormon dish. Basically they're hash browns mixed with cream of chicken soup with cheese and cornflakes on top."

"Cornflakes?"

"Cornflakes," she said. She looked around the room. "You're making progress."

"Slowly. The front room is more work than I expected."

"You could fill a Dumpster just with that."

"I did find an old record player and some records."

She smiled. "That's exciting. Finding old music is like running into an old friend, isn't it?"

I nodded. "I like that. Do you mind if I eat?"

"No. That's why I brought it."

I got a plate and silverware, dished up some food, and brought it over to the table. "Did you want anything?"

"Heavens no. I've been pilfering calories all day."

"Well, thank you for thinking of me."

She waited until I sat down, then said, "How's it coming?"

"It's taking longer than I thought it would."

"I know. When you said you would only be a few days, I wondered if you knew what you'd gotten yourself into."

I lifted a full fork. "Funeral potatoes?"

"Funeral potatoes," she confirmed.

I took a bite. They were good. "Well, at least I don't have to do anything with the yard."

"Until the last few years you wouldn't have had to. Your mother spent a lot of time gardening. I think it was her therapy. Her yard was beautiful. That was before she stopped going outside. After that . . ." She didn't finish.

"The pyracantha bushes are out of control."

"The red berries do look pretty against the white snow, though, don't they? In the spring the birds get drunk on them."

"Birds get drunk?"

"They roll around like sailors on a weekend pass. It's kind of funny to watch," she said. "And in the summer, the berries are always good for the bees when the flowers start to dry out."

"My mother once sent me out to pick pyracantha berries to make them into jelly," I said. "I don't know if it was intentional or not, but she didn't bother to tell me that the berries were poisonous. Fortunately, they were bitter and didn't taste good, so I only ate a handful and ended up throwing them up."

Elyse frowned. "I'm sure it wasn't intentional," she said softly. "I've made jelly with those berries before. If you prepare it right and you add enough sugar, it tastes like apple jelly and you cook the toxins out. Of course anything is palatable with enough sugar."

"Speaking of palatable, this is all delicious."

"I'm glad you like it. I forgot to mention, there's a piece

of apple pie in there. I wrapped it in foil. I had to stash away a piece for you or else it would have been eaten. I guess funerals make people hungry."

I was really surprised at her consideration. "I love apple pie. Thank you again for thinking of me."

"My pleasure," she said. "So you came over to the house earlier."

I looked up. "How did you know that?"

"We have neighbors with too much time on their hands. They said you were with a young lady."

"Yes, I was."

"You don't need surveillance cameras when you've got neighbors like mine. If you had driven to my house, they would have given me the license plate number. Did you need something?"

"I had a question for you. I don't know if you would remember, but when I was little, did we have a young pregnant woman live with us?"

Her brow furrowed. "A pregnant woman? No." She slowly shook her head. "I could always be wrong, but it was always just the four of you." Her answer made me sad. "Why do you ask?"

"The young woman I was with, she came by to see if anyone remembered her mother living here. She said she thought her mother had lived here when she was pregnant with her."

Suddenly Elyse's expression changed. "Come to think of it, there was a young woman staying with you for a short while. She was pretty, had dark, almost black hair. I think she came a few months before your brother passed."

"Why was she living with us?"

"I don't know. It may be that her family was very religious and embarrassed. That used to happen a lot in my day. She stayed until she gave birth, then left a short time after that without her baby. She never came back. I don't know how I could have forgotten that, except it was such a difficult time, with your brother passing."

"Do you remember her name?"

Again her brow furrowed, then she said, "No. It was too long ago. I didn't ever really see much of her. She didn't go out much, or it was after dark when she did, like she was hiding. I usually just saw her when she would answer the door. She helped out around the house, did dishes and cooked meals. Looked after you." She looked at me. "Your father would know. Is it important?"

"It is to my friend."

"You could always just give your father a call."

It was strange to think of that possibility. In the alienation of my youth he had always seemed to me like a mythical creature.

"I haven't talked to him since he left. I don't even know where he lives."

"He lives in Mesa, Arizona. It's a suburb of Phoenix."

"I've been there," I said. "Several times. On book tour. There's a famous bookstore near there in Scottsdale—The Poisoned Pen." I wondered how close I had unknowingly come to my father's house.

"I have his contact information," Elyse said. "I spoke with him at your mother's funeral. He gave me his phone number. He also asked me to contact him if I saw you."

I don't know what surprised me more, that he went to my mother's funeral or that he asked about me. "Did you?"

"Not yet. I thought I'd talk to you first."

"May I have that number?"

"Of course. I don't have my phone with me, but if you give me your phone number, I will call you with the number when I get back to the house. It's one of those new smartphones. I know there's a way to share things, but I don't know how to do it. I'll just call you with it."

"I'll write down my number," I said. I walked over to the cupboard and found a pen I had left in there and wrote down my cell phone number. "Here you go," I said, handing it to her.

She looked at it and smiled. "Jacob Churcher's personal phone number. Think I could sell this on eBay?"

I smiled back. "If you can get anything out of that, you're welcome to it."

She laughed. "You're still delightful. Well, I best be getting back. I've been on my feet all day and I need to get them up."

I stood with her and walked her to the door. "Thank you for dinner," I said. "And for the information."

"You're very welcome. Have you ever wondered if people come into our lives for a reason?"

"I can't say that I have," I said.

"Well, you might just give it a thought." She turned and walked out the door. I shut the door behind her.

My mind was reeling. How could I not have remembered Rachel's mother? Then again, I was young and I had other things to worry about. Then a thought struck me. *Could she have been the woman I was dreaming about? Was that why Rachel seemed so familiar?*

After I finished eating, I cleaned the dishes and went back into the front room to decide whether or not I wanted to dive back into the mess or just call it a night. I received a text from Elyse with my father's contact info.

As I looked at the address, I had a strong desire to see him. I played around with the idea of driving to Arizona as I drove back to my hotel.

That night I dreamt of the woman again. Only this time the dream was more real than ever. I could feel her soft hands on my face. Her lips, kissing my cheek. I was crying. I don't know why, but I was. And she was gently telling me that everything would be okay.

CHAPTER *Twelve*

December 15

I woke excited to tell Rachel what I'd found out about her mother. At least I think it was that. It had been a while since I'd looked forward to seeing any woman, engaged or not.

I got to the house early, even though I'd stopped and picked up a couple of lattes. As I pulled up, Rachel's red Honda Accord was already there, idling in front of the mailbox. When she saw me she turned off her car and got out. She was also carrying coffee cups. She laughed when she saw me. "Looks like we'll be well caffeinated."

We made our way into the house and took our beverages into the kitchen.

"I didn't know what you liked to drink," Rachel said, taking off her jacket. She was dressed in denim jeans and a black V-necked tee that accentuated her petite yet curvaceous form. "So I got you something sweet, their signature hot chocolate, and something bitter, the caffè misto. You pick first. I can go either way."

"Sweet or bitter. That ought to be an easy choice." I took the caffè. As I looked at her, I thought she was even more gorgeous than I remembered. "I got us a couple of pumpkin spice lattes."

"Perfect. We can drink them all. Then work much faster."

"Before we start, I need to tell you something. You'd better sit down."

"That is so cliché," she said, sitting down. She looked anxious. "Is it something bad? Did I do something wrong?"

I thought her second question was kind of telling. "No. I have good news. The elderly lady I told you about remembered your mother."

Rachel screamed. Then she came around the table and hugged me. When we parted, she looked me in the eyes. "What did she say?"

"She said a few months before my brother died, there was a young pregnant woman who came to stay with us."

"Did she know her name?"

"No," I said. "I'm sorry."

The excitement left her face. "Then I still have nothing."

"But she said my father would."

"You said that's a dead end."

"It was. But she gave me my father's contact information. He lives in Mesa, Arizona." I took a deep breath. "I'm thinking of driving to Arizona," I said. "Maybe it's time I confronted him. I'll ask him about your mother as well."

"Thank you." She looked down a moment, then blurted out, "May I go with you?"

I looked at her in surprise. "You want to go with me to Arizona?"

"I'd like to talk to your father in person."

"Will your fiancé be okay with that?"

She frowned. "Yeah, I'll need to talk to him about it. He won't be happy."

"You've been looking for your mother for half your life. Why wouldn't he be happy for you?"

"Because I told him that I would be back by today. He's not exactly spontaneous. And he has a work social he wanted me to help cook for." She breathed out in exasperation. "I'll talk to him. In the meantime, we have a lot of work to do. Come on." She grabbed a coffee and took it into the front room.

The room looked less daunting with someone helping me. A few minutes after we started working, Rachel said, "That is such a beautiful piano. Is it really a Steinway?"

I nodded. "It's a pearl in this oyster. My mother's uncle left it to her when he died. I was really young when she got it, so I don't remember life without it."

"Can you play it?"

"A little," I said. "I used to be pretty good."

"Play me something."

"All right." I sat down on the bench and began to play James Taylor's "Fire and Rain." When I finished, I turned around on the bench. "Well?"

"That was beautiful," she said. "I love that song."

"Me too. It has soul."

"Like you," she said.

We went back to work.

I came across three boxes filled with piano music, most of which I remembered. I dusted off the boxes and stacked them by the piano to send home with the instrument.

I found some more vinyl albums of my parents that I had grown up with. The soundtracks to *South Pacific* and *Camelot*, Herb Alpert's *Whipped Cream and Other Delights*; the picture of the girl on the cover had wrought havoc on my potent teenage male hormones. I lifted the Herb Alpert album to show Rachel. "Ever seen this? The cover is pretty iconic."

She shook her head. "She's pretty. Can we play it?"

"Yes we can." I put on the album, and the sound of brass filled the room.

"This music makes me happy," she said.

I looked at the simple joy on her face and also smiled.

Around one, Rachel drove to a nearby deli to get us something for lunch. I was able to fill three more trash bags by the time she got back. I saw her walking up to the door and I opened it for her.

"Thank you," she said, walking in. She carried the food to the kitchen table. "Sorry that took so long. There was a long line. I also got us a couple of Cokes," she said, handing me a bottle.

We sat down at the table. When I looked up, Rachel had her head bowed in prayer. A moment later she looked up and smiled at me.

"Do you always pray?" I asked.

"I always give thanks," she said.

I couldn't remember the last time I'd prayed.

We both started eating. A minute later Rachel said, "So, I called Brandon while I was waiting in line at the deli."

"And?"

"He wasn't happy." She groaned lightly. "Actually, that's putting it mildly. He was livid. He tried to talk me out of it."

"Because of me?"

"No. He didn't want me to be gone any longer. And he was worried about the cost of gas."

"He was worried about the gas money but not about you driving to Arizona with another man?"

She looked at me sheepishly. "I didn't tell him about you."

"Okay, so he was worried about gas money but not about you driving *alone* to another state."

"He cares," she said. "Men just aren't expressive like that."

"Don't pin that on us," I said. "Most men are highly protective."

"If it was you, would you have been upset?"

"If it was me, I would have gone with you."

She breathed out softly. "Well, we're going. I'll deal with the fallout later. I shouldn't have called him. It's easier to ask forgiveness than permission." She frowned. "The thing is, I'm really easy for him to manipulate, because I feel guilty a lot. I feel guilty about everything. It's like this crushing weight on me. I can't even take the last cookie on the plate without feeling guilty." She shook her head. "Brandon doesn't feel guilt very much. I once asked him why he didn't feel guilty like I did and he just laughed."

"Are you sure you want to go?"

"I feel like I need to. And I feel like I can't let him stop me from doing this. If I missed this opportunity, I might not forgive myself. I might not forgive *him*. I can't be sure that I wouldn't always resent him. And that wouldn't be good for our marriage."

"No, it wouldn't," I said. "So, it will take about nine hours from here. If we leave by noon, we could make it by night."

"We could leave earlier."

"I would, except I can't leave until after the piano movers come; but we'll leave right after."

"Okay," she said. "I'll be packed."

CHAPTER
Thirteen

By six o'clock we had cleared out more than half the room. We stopped at my mother's doll collection, about six boxes filled with American Girl dolls and accessories. I don't know when she had started purchasing them, but since she'd only had boys, they were clearly just for her. Rachel said that if I was planning on throwing the dolls away, she wanted them.

We were both getting tired and hungry, so I locked up the house and took Rachel to dinner at an Italian restaurant I'd driven past a few times. I guessed that the restaurant must have been pretty good since the parking lot and dining room were always full.

The hostess led us to a small, candlelit table in the corner of the room. I slid out the chair for Rachel, then sat down across from her. She looked a little anxious.

"Are you okay?" I asked.

"I'm fine," she said. As she looked at the menu, she looked even more upset.

"Are you sure you're okay?"

She nodded unconvincingly.

"Is it that you're uncomfortable being out with me in public?"

She set down her menu. "No. Otherwise, I never would have offered to go on a road trip with a complete stranger."

"I'm not a *complete* stranger."

She grinned. "You're not?"

"For the sake of argument, do we ever really know anyone?"

She laughed. "Now you're going existential on me. You and I don't have history."

"But we just sorted through decades of history together."

"That's true."

"And we both like James Taylor."

"Yes. That is telling."

"Then what are you worried about?"

"Actually, it's just that this place is too expensive. We can go somewhere else."

"No, no. It looks good."

"We'll go Dutch."

"I can afford it," I said.

"I just don't want to take advantage of your kindness."

"That's refreshing."

"What?"

"Someone who doesn't want to take advantage of me."

She paused for a moment. "I think people like you probably get taken advantage of pretty often."

"People like me?" I said.

"Kind people."

I took a deep breath. "Maybe I am a complete stranger."

She smiled, then lifted her menu, pausing a moment to look over it. "Have you ever had—I can't pronounce it—gu-no-chee?"

"It's pronounced *nyok-ee*. The *chi* is pronounced hard, like *k*. It comes from the Italian word *nocchio*, which literally means a knot in wood."

"So, it's hard to pronounce, but is it good?"

"It usually is. American restaurants don't always get it right."

"I'll take my chances. What are you having?"

"I think I'll have the spaghetti vongole, that's spaghetti with clams. I'd recommend the Chianti to go with your meal."

"Are you trying to impress me?"

I set down the menu. "Yes. Is it working?"

"I'm very impressed. I'm just a small-town girl. The Pasta Factory in St. George is the best Italian in our area."

Just then the waiter came up to our table with water and bread. After we had ordered, I said, "So, tell me about yourself."

"What would you like to know?"

"All of it." I meant it. I wanted to know everything I could about this woman.

"Okay. So where do I start?"

"At the beginning," I said. "Then go through the middle and end at the end."

She smiled. "Like I said, I live just a little northwest of St. George in Ivins. Have you heard of Ivins?"

"No."

"It's just a little place. My parents moved there twenty-five years ago. It's beautiful, with the red rock and Snow Canyon, but when we moved there, it was mostly just poor people and farmers. We were sort of poor. I'm sure my parents moved there because it was cheap and isolated.

"It's changed. Now there's a lot of money coming in and big developments growing all around us. We used to be out in the middle of nowhere; now we're in a subdivision with big homes. Most of their garages are bigger than our house. The old people got pushed out and the new people moved in.

"My father grumbles about it a lot. What really gets him is that it's becoming kind of an artist enclave. 'Educated idiots,' he calls them. I bought him a bumper sticker that read *I lived in Ivins before Ivins was cool*. He never put it on his car."

I grinned. "Do you have siblings?"

"No. I'm an only child. My parents are older. They're retired now, in their late seventies. They were unable to have children, so it wasn't until they were in their forties that they adopted me. I was adopted at birth. My parents are pretty tight-lipped anyway, but they kept the whole thing secret, so I didn't even know until I was sixteen that I was adopted. I suspected it before then, but I didn't ask."

"Why did you suspect it?"

"We don't look much alike. Mostly my eyes . . ."

"You have beautiful eyes," I said.

She smiled shyly. "Thank you. You're embarrassing me. But thank you."

"You're welcome."

She seemed a little flustered. "I was saying, I don't look like them, but more telling than that was our personalities. I don't know how much is nature versus nurture, but in the personality department, I'm completely different from my parents. I'm kind of a free spirit and they're hyper religious. Like, my mother could have been a nun and my dad is practically ascetic."

"That must have been difficult for you, growing up that way."

"I disappoint them a lot. I suppose that's where the guilt thing comes in. Even my name."

"Rachel's a pretty name," I said.

"They named me Rachel because it's a Bible name. It means ewe. A female sheep. I was named after an animal."

I laughed. "Animal or not, it's still a pretty name."

"Thank you. They named me that because of the Bible verse in Matthew that said God will put the sheep on the right and the goats on the left."

"I'm a goat," I said.

"Well, if I'm a sheep, I'm the black one. When I was fourteen, I was with some friends in the St. George Mall when a man handed me his business card and asked if I would be interested in modeling, like in magazines or TV commercials. I was really excited. But when I showed my mother the man's card, she went crazy. She said that I needed to repent and that vanity was of the devil and all models are going to hell."

"That might be true," I said.

She looked at me, unsure if I was being serious or not.

"I was joking," I said. "But I've dated a few models . . ."

She grinned. "Then you should know."

I laughed. "I should know *better*, that is. When did you find out you were adopted?"

"When I was sixteen, a friend at school asked me how old I was when I was adopted. I said, 'I'm not adopted.' She just looked at me like I was crazy. She said, 'Really? Are you sure?' That night I asked my parents. They didn't have to say a thing. I knew immediately from their reactions that I was. I asked them why they hadn't told me sooner and my mother said that they were waiting until I was older, because they were afraid that I might feel different or unwanted by my birth mother."

"Is that why you started looking for your birth parents?"

"Not really. I asked my parents about them, but they said it was a sealed adoption and that even they didn't know who the mother was. They said that they knew the woman wasn't married and that the father wasn't any part of the deal." Rachel grinned. "I mean, he had to be *some* part of the deal. It's not like I was an immaculate conception."

"Not likely," I said.

I looked at her for a moment, then said, "Why do you want to find her?"

"*There's* a question," she said. "I don't know if I could put words to it. It's like finding yourself." She looked at me. "What about your mother? You said you weren't close."

"No. I moved out of her house when I was sixteen. This is the first time I've been back since then."

"You didn't see your mother before she died?"

"No."

"Do you wish you had?"

I thought over the question. "I don't know. Part of me does. Part of me wishes I could see her and she'd apologize. But more likely than not I just would have been disappointed again. She probably would have asked me who I was."

"I'm sorry."

I sighed. "It's nothing. I mean, it is, but it's history now."

"So why go through the house if all there is is pain?"

"I'm still looking for clues."

"Clues to what?"

I looked at her thoughtfully. "There's something I haven't told you about. For years I've had these dreams of me as a child and a woman holding me, loving me. I've wondered who she was or whether she even existed." I swallowed. "Now I'm wondering if she was your mother."

Just then the waiter walked up to the table carrying a tray. "Gnocchi with sage butter." He set the plate down in front of Rachel. "And the spaghetti vongole for you." He set another plate in front of me.

He turned to Rachel. "Would you like some Parmesan cheese on that?"

"Yes, please." He grated cheese on top of it.

"There you go. Can I get you anything else?"

"Could you get me a glass of Chianti?" I said.

"Absolutely."

He walked away.

"Buon appetito," I said.

We ate for a moment in silence. Rachel spoke first. "This is really good. Do you want to try some?"

"Please."

She speared a couple of dumplings and held her fork out for me to eat. I ate them off the fork. "Those are good. Would you like to try mine?"

She looked at it a moment, then said, "I'm not a big oyster fan."

"They're not oysters, they're clams," I said.

"To-may-to, to-maw-to," she replied.

"Then I'll keep my shellfish to myself." I looked at her and added, *"Shellfishly."*

She laughed. "That was an awful pun."

"That's the nature of a pun—the more awful the better. Bad enough and it's good."

"You almost turned the corner on that one," she said. "I can see why you're a writer."

The waiter set the glass of wine on the table. "There you are, sir."

"Thank you."

He walked away. I took a sip, then set down my glass. "Do you like wine?"

"I've never tried it."

"You've never tasted wine?"

"No. I told you, my parents were . . . strict. Alcohol was forbidden."

"But you must have had opportunities. When they weren't around?"

"I tried beer at my high school graduation party," she said.

"You are definitely going to hell."

She laughed. "It *tasted* like hell. I didn't like it."

"It's an acquired taste. Like . . . clams."

"And oysters."

"And oysters. What do they say, it was a brave man who first ate an oyster."

"How do you know it wasn't a brave woman?"

"Because women have more sense than that." I took another bite of my pasta, then said, "Tell me about Braydon."

"Brandon."

"Sorry. Do your parents approve of Brandon?"

"Approve? I think they like him more than they like me."

"Why is that?"

"He's just like them. He's kind of . . . severe." She looked at me. "I shouldn't have said that. He's a good guy."

"What does he do?"

"He works for a sporting supply company."

"He's a jock?"

She burst out laughing. "No. He's a bookkeeper. He weighs almost the same as I do. Unfortunately, his job doesn't pay much, which is why he's so upset about me not working. But someday he wants to open his own store."

"A sporting store?"

"No. A video-game store. He plays a lot of video games. That's his release."

"And you?"

"I don't like video games."

I laughed. "I meant, what about *your* career."

"I like being a dental assistant. Someday I want to be a mother. Does that sound unambitious?"

"The world needs more good mothers."

"How about you?" she asked.

"I'd make a terrible mother."

She laughed. "I meant your career. I know you're a writer. Is that how you make your living, or do you have side gigs as well?"

I hid my smile. "Well, I used to work for a healthcare company, writing newsletters and press releases. But now I sell enough books to keep a roof over my head."

She nodded. "I wish I could do something creative for a living. But I'd first have to have some creativity." She ate a little, then said, "Before I go back home, I need to do some Christmas shopping. There are so many great stores in Salt Lake. How about you? Have you finished your Christmas shopping?"

"I haven't even started yet. I'll probably do some shopping when I go back to New York."

"Why are you going to New York?"

"To meet with my . . ." I stopped. "My friend."

"Oh." She looked at me. "A woman friend?"

I thought I detected a note of jealousy in her voice. Maybe I was just being hopeful. "You could say that."

There was a brief, awkward pause. "I've never been to New York City," she said wistfully.

"It's a great city. Especially at Christmastime. It's

crowded, but it has an energy you won't find anywhere else." Then I added, "Except maybe in Ivins."

"Yeah, right. I've always wanted to see New York. I'd probably just get lost."

"You just need the right guide," I said.

"Like you?"

I smiled. "Exactly like me."

We finished eating around ten. The restaurant was trying to close down and I could tell they were eager for us to leave. Especially when they started mopping the floor next to us. Finally we drove back to the house. I pulled up behind Rachel's car and turned off the ignition. Rachel turned to me. "That was a really good restaurant." She grinned. "Even if they tried to throw us out."

"The company wasn't bad either."

She smiled.

"Thanks for all your help today," I said.

"It was my pleasure."

"When I decided to come down, I didn't plan on having company. You are . . . enjoyable."

"Enjoyable?"

"Today wasn't miserable."

"*Miserable* is a long way from enjoyable."

"Exactly," I said.

She laughed. "About tomorrow. Are you sure it's okay if I go with you?"

"Of course it's okay with me. Like I said, I like your company. Are you having second thoughts?"

"No. I just wish I could be more straightforward with Brandon without him getting so angry about everything." She looked at me. "How about you? Are you worried about seeing your father?"

"A little. I really don't know how it will go. I guess I'll find out."

"When do the piano movers come?"

"They're supposed to be there at eleven. But I'm going over earlier. I wanted to get some more done before they get there."

"Name the time," she said.

"Is eight too early?"

"Eight it is."

"I'll bring the coffee," I said. "And some muffins?"

"I love muffins. Thank you. Good night."

"Good night," I said.

She leaned forward as if to kiss me, then stopped. Even in the limited light I could see her blush. "I'm so sorry, I don't know why I did that."

"It's just habit," I said. "No worries."

"Sorry. I'll see you at eight." She looked flustered as she got out and walked to her car. She looked back and smiled before climbing in. I lightly waved to her. She started her car, then did a U-turn in the road and drove away.

As I watched her go, I was definitely feeling something for her. Wrong or not, I wished that we had kissed.

CHAPTER

Fourteen

December 16

I woke early. Too early. A quarter to five. It had been a restless night. My mind was too active, spinning like a roulette wheel, the ball occasionally dropping on different topics of intrigue: encountering my father, my mother, the house, Rachel's mother, and Rachel.

A half hour later I gave up on sleep and went downstairs to the fitness center and ran on the treadmill for an hour, then went back to my room and packed for our trip. An hour later I left for the house.

I stopped at a Starbucks for coffee and blueberry muffins. Even though I was twenty minutes early, Rachel was already there at the house, smoke rising from her car's tailpipe.

She smiled at me as I walked toward her carrying our coffee and muffins. "Good morning," she said. "How did you sleep?"

"Awful. I had strange dreams."

"About what?"

"Things." I handed her a coffee, and she took a sip.

"I'm sorry," she said again. "I had strange dreams too. Only mine were nice."

"About what?"

"Things," she said, with a curious smile on her face. She turned and walked ahead of me through the snow to the front porch. When we reached the front door, I handed Rachel my cup, took the house key from my pocket, unlocked the door, and opened it. I followed her inside.

The room was warm, and I could hear the sound of the furnace blowing. I turned on the lights, then walked over and opened the blinds.

"It doesn't smell as bad as it did yesterday," Rachel said behind me.

"The magic of Lysol."

"And we have a full three hours before the movers get here. We might actually finish." She set her coffee down on a cleared end table. "So, after dinner, I went back to my hotel and decided to see if I could find your books on Amazon."

"And?"

"I found five of them, all major bestsellers, with thousands and thousands of fans. Then I looked up your Facebook page. You have like a million followers. I was so embarrassed."

"Why?"

"I kept asking how you made a living. You didn't tell

me you were a famous author and have sold millions of books."

"If you have to tell people you're famous, you're not."

She laughed. "You could have told me."

"Why? So you could act differently?"

"No. Because it's who you are."

"No, it's not really who I am. It's my image. You've seen more of who I am digging through this junk than my readers will ever know."

She nodded. "I believe that."

"It's nice to not have to be author Jacob Churcher, just Jacob."

"I understand that," she said. "I'm sorry. I hope I didn't ruin anything."

"We'll be okay," I said, smiling. "We've got enough ground beneath us."

"You mean because I liked you *before* I found out you were famous?"

I liked the comment. "Something like that."

"Well, how about, I'll still like you *even though* you're famous."

"So that's how it is," I said.

She smiled. "Yep. That's how it is. Your fifteen minutes of fame are over. Now get back to work."

I grinned. "Now you sound like my agent."

I was sitting on the ground in front of the piano bench going through a box of Christmas decorations when

Rachel said, "I think you're going to want to see this." I looked over. She was holding an open box.

"What is it?"

She handed me the box. "It's a diary."

I took the box from her. Inside was a leather book about the size of one of my paperback novels. The word DIARY was embossed in gold into its leather face. I opened it up. The lined paper was old and the handwriting that covered it was graceful and feminine and mostly in red ink. I started to read.

June 11, 1986

Dear Diary,

I've started this new diary, since I'm starting a new life. I'm afraid to say that nothing will be the same after today. I'm leaving home tomorrow morning. I don't know when I'll be back, or if they'll even let me back. My parents are sending me away to Salt Lake City to have my baby. The woman who is facilitating my stay says that I would usually first meet the people I'll be staying with, but my parents are rushing this because my mother says I'm beginning to show, even though I'm only eleven weeks along. Last night at dinner my parents argued over whether they should tell people that I went to live at my aunt's house or went away to a special school. They chose the latter alibi, as family members would see through the other. It's the story I've been told to stick to. They're ashamed of me. And I have this baby that I'm bringing into the world in shame. I'm so sorry, little one. I still haven't heard from Peter. I miss him.

Noel

"Noel," I said. I looked up at Rachel. "I think your mother's name was Noel. I think this is your mother's diary."

Rachel stood. "It's my mother's?" She practically ran back over to my side. "Her name is Noel?"

There were three photographs inside the book. I lifted them out. The first was a picture of my family. My mother, father, Charles, and me. I looked like I was about four, so it must have been fairly close to the time my brother died. My parents looked so young. I was sitting on my mother's lap. She looked different than I remembered her. Besides being noticeably younger, there was light in her eyes. My parents were smiling. It seemed so foreign to me.

The next picture was of a young man. He looked about nineteen or twenty. He was sitting on a motorcycle. He had long, black hair and wore a leather bomber jacket. He had a look of confidence in his eyes.

"I wonder who that is," I said.

I lifted the next picture and froze. It was *her*. The woman in my dreams. She was real, right there in color. She was in the photograph with my father. He was standing in the kitchen about to blow out the candles on a birthday cake. To his side sat a young woman with a slightly protruding stomach. She was holding me on her lap.

Rachel gasped. "That's her. That's my mother . . ."

I handed her the picture.

"Oh my . . ." Her eyes welled up. She covered her mouth with her hand. Then she began to cry.

I let her cry for a moment, then put my arm around her. "Are you okay?"

"I can't believe I'm finally seeing her. I look like her." She held the picture in front of her face like it was a mirror. She looked stunned.

"You have the same facial features."

She wiped more tears away. "I can't believe this." Then she leaned her face into my shoulder and just broke down crying. I put my arms around her, gently rubbing my hand over her back to comfort her. She kept saying over and over, "She's real. She's real."

I shuffled back to the second picture. "I wonder if that's your father."

She took the picture from me and just stared at it. Then she turned it over. Scrawled on the back in the same handwriting as the diary was one word:

Peter

I held up the photo and looked at Rachel. "There's a resemblance," I said.

More tears welled up in her eyes. When she could speak, she said, "I have to see her. I have so many questions."

I took a deep breath. "Now I know why you looked so familiar to me the first time I met you. Your mother is the girl in my dreams."

CHAPTER *Fifteen*

The woman in my dreams existed. In a way, Rachel and I were having the same experience: both of us had wondered for most of our lives about the same woman, then suddenly there she was, captured on film. It was surreal—like seeing a picture of Bigfoot or the Loch Ness Monster.

I started to read Noel's diary out loud.

June 18, 1986

Dear Diary,

The home I have been sent to belongs to a family named the Churchers. It's small but comfortable. They're nice. The man, Scott, is a social worker, which is why I was sent here. He's kind. The woman, Ruth, is polite to me but quiet. I don't know if she really wants me in the house. They have two young boys: a very active eight-year-old named Charles, and a sweet little four-year-old named Jacob. His middle name is Christian. Christian Churcher. I think that's kind of cute. He's adorable and immediately took to me. I think we will be good friends. Still no word from Peter. Where is he?

Noel

I looked over at Rachel, who sat rapt, clearly eager to hear more. I turned the page.

June 25, 1986

Dear Diary,

Peter is gone. I called my friend Diane. She saw him with another girl. Rebecca. I feel like the victim of a hit-and-run. How could he do this? He said he loved me. Of course he did. He wanted me.

I just finished the first trimester of my pregnancy. Time is moving very slowly. I have very strange cravings. The other day I wanted to eat the dust on the windowsill. I feel like I'm losing my mind. Not all is bad. I was in my room crying, and little Jacob walked up to me. He laid his forehead against mine. It's like he knows I'm hurting. He just stood there. I took him in my arms, and he nestled into me. It's almost like he came at this time to show me the potential joy of motherhood.

Noel

As a writer, I found it surreal to be reading about myself in the third person, like a character in someone else's story. Yet the truth of what I was reading resonated like a thinly veiled memory.

There was a knock at the door. I looked out the window and saw a large white truck with a picture of a piano keyboard running the length of its trailer. I handed the journal to Rachel.

"Looks like the piano movers are here," I said. I got up and walked over to the door and opened it. A broad Polynesian man stood on the front porch. He wore a black beanie, a hoodie, and leather gloves. His breath froze in the air in front of him. "We're here for the piano."

"It's right in here. Come in."

He stepped inside the room. "That's a big one," he said. "Steinway. Nice." He stepped back out the door and waved at the truck. The truck's driver pulled forward out into the road, then backed up to the end of the driveway. Then, gathering a little speed, the truck broke through the tall bank of snow into the driveway, stopping about ten feet before the Dumpster. The driver shut down the truck.

"Grab a snow shovel," the man on my porch shouted to the driver as he climbed out.

"Sorry," I said. "I should have shoveled, but I don't have one. I don't live here. We're just cleaning up."

"No worries, man."

It took the piano movers about an hour to wrap the piano in cellophane and padding, attach it to a gurney, carry it outside, and load it into their truck. I gave them my home address and the number of my housekeeper, Lilia, to call when they reached the city. Then I called her and arranged for her to prepare a place for the piano in my living room and to meet the movers at the house and let them in.

After they were gone, I looked back at Rachel. "Ready to go?"

She hadn't stopped reading from the journal. "Can I bring this with us?"

"Of course."

She tucked the diary carefully under her arm.

I turned off the kitchen lights and locked the back door, then turned down the thermostat. As I walked back into the front room, someone knocked at the door. I opened it to see Elyse standing in the cold. She wore a long, red wool coat and boots.

"I'm glad I caught you," she said. "I saw the moving truck."

"They were just taking the piano. I'm having them deliver it to my home."

She stopped and looked at Rachel. "We haven't met."

"I'm Rachel Garner."

Elyse extended her hand. "I'm Elyse Foster. I live just two doors east from here, but I think you've been to my house."

"Yes, ma'am."

"I remember your mother being beautiful too."

"You remember my mother?"

"Only a little. She wasn't here long, and it was a very long time ago."

"Come in," I said.

"Thank you." She smiled a little as she walked over to the couch. "I always liked this couch." She looked at me. "When I saw the moving truck pulling out, I was afraid that you might be leaving today."

"Actually, I am."

Her face fell. "Are you going back home?"

"No. I'm driving to Phoenix to see my father."

"Oh." She looked thoughtful. "He'll be very happy to see you."

"I hope so."

"I know he will."

"How do you know that?"

"Because he told me that he was very disappointed that you weren't at the funeral." She forced a smile. "So do you know what you're going to say when you meet him?"

"No idea. I've got the drive time to figure that out." I looked at Rachel. "I know that I plan to ask him how to find Rachel's mother."

"He might know that," she said, glancing at Rachel.

"So do you have any advice?" I asked. "For how I should approach my father?"

She thought for a moment, then said, "With grace."

I looked at her quizzically. "You think he deserves it?"

"If he deserved it, it wouldn't be grace, now would it?" She looked at me. "It's easy to see how things should have gone after the fact. He didn't know how your mother was. She didn't turn the way she did until several years after he was gone. He never would have allowed it."

"You know that?"

"I knew him. He was very protective of you boys. That's why he was so broken by Charles's death." She sighed. "Well, I better not keep you any longer. Do you plan to come back here before you go home?"

"Yes. I still have some legal work."

"Very good. Then please stop by and let me know how

everything goes. I'll pray that it all goes well and you find what you're looking for."

"Thank you."

She looked past me to Rachel. "Good luck to you, dear. And Merry Christmas."

"Thank you. Merry Christmas to you too."

She turned and walked out the door. I helped Elyse down the stairs, then went back inside where Rachel was sitting on the sofa.

"What do you think?" I asked.

"She's nice. It's just weird thinking that she's seen my mother. It's like these people who have near-death experiences and come back and say they've seen God."

"I'm pretty sure that your mother's not God."

"No. But they do have something in common."

"What's that?"

"I've never seen either of them."

CHAPTER

Sixteen

July 2, 1986

Dear Diary,

I'm having a little morning sickness. Actually, a lot. I throw up a lot. It's been three weeks, and I haven't heard from my parents. I know that I've messed up, but why are they not even talking to me? Then again, based on our last conversations, maybe this is a good thing.

Noel

I took Rachel's suitcase from her car and put it in mine, and then we drove separately downtown to the Grand America. We switched cars so I could park hers below in the parking garage. Then I took the elevator up to meet Rachel.

She was standing in the middle of the spacious lobby next to a massive display of flowers, looking at all the Christmas decorations. A young woman was near the back of the lobby playing "Greensleeves" on a harp. "This is a really nice hotel," Rachel said. "Do you always stay here?"

"I haven't been to Utah since I was a teenager. It didn't even exist then," I said.

"Their Christmas decorations are beautiful."

"Down that corridor there are window displays and a massive gingerbread house. Maybe when we get back we can look at the decorations."

She smiled. "I'd like that."

"It's a date," I said.

She looked at me.

"Well, not really a date. More like an appointment."

"Appointment sounds cold," she said. "How about an engagement?"

I grinned. "No, you already have one of those. Let's stick with date. As in a platonic hookup."

"You're the wordsmith."

"Should we get some lunch before we leave or should we just grab something on the way?"

"Let's get something on our way," she said. "We should try to make it before dark."

We walked outside and the valet handed me the key to my car. "Let's get out of here."

The I-15 southbound on-ramp was only a few blocks from the hotel. We drove south through the Salt Lake valley into Utah County through Provo, almost a hundred miles before we stopped at the town of Nephi for gas. We hadn't talked much, as Rachel had been reading from her mother's diary most of the way, and I didn't want to interrupt her.

After filling the car with gas, I went inside the mart and bought a couple of energy shots and beer nuts, then went back to the car. "It's past two. Let's get some lunch," I said. "What sounds good?"

"I don't care," Rachel said. All around the gas station were the typical fast-food joints. Almost adjoining the gas station was an independent restaurant. "What about that place? J. C. Mickelson's?"

"Cars in the parking lot," I said. "Must be good."

"It's got your initials," she said. "Maybe that's a good sign."

Inside, the restaurant looked as homegrown as it sounded. There were model trains that drove around on a suspended track that ran the perimeter of the restaurant.

I ordered a French dip sandwich with a baked potato and an Arnold Palmer to drink. Rachel ordered soup and salad with a homemade scone served with honey butter, which started a brief conversation on the true definition of scone. What is called a scone in Utah is really just deep-fried bread dough—what they call elephant ears in the South or fry bread, skillet bread, or sopaipillas in most other places. Whatever you call them, two came with Rachel's soup and we shared them.

It was a quarter past three before we were on the road again. Our route took us south on I-15 until about twelve miles past Beaver (where a billboard advertised the best-tasting water in America), east on I-20 through Bear Valley to I-89, then south down past the turnoffs for Bryce Canyon and Zion National Park, through Kanab, then east and across the border into Page, Arizona, where we stopped for gas. It was past eight o'clock, so we got some dinner. Actually, it was seven o'clock since we had gained an hour crossing the border.

We stopped at a small Mexican restaurant before continuing south on 89 through the Navajo Indian Reservation to Flagstaff.

Even though Flagstaff was only a little more than two hours outside of Phoenix, I decided that it was still too far to drive. It was already past one. Rachel had been asleep for several hours, and the kick from the energy shots I'd downed had faded.

I stopped at the first hotel I came to—a Holiday Inn. Rachel woke as I parked underneath the hotel's lighted front entrance. She looked cute, her hair slightly mussed and her eyes heavy with sleep.

"Are we here?" Her voice was scratchy. Morning voice.

"We're in Flagstaff," I said. "I'm too tired to drive."

I opened my door. "Just stay here. I'll make sure they have rooms." I got out of the car and walked inside. The front desk was abandoned and I had to ring a bell for service. Almost immediately a weary-looking clerk walked out to greet me. His eyes were bloodshot and he looked like I had woken him. "May I help you?"

"Do you have two rooms available?"

"Sure. King or queen?"

"Doesn't matter. Just as long as it's quiet."

"It's quiet."

I gave him my credit card and ID, and he produced two plastic keys for me.

"Thank you." I walked out and got back in the car. "They have rooms." I parked the car and got our two suitcases from the backseat. Rachel was practically sleepwalking. Actually, she was acting drunk.

"Come on." I led her to the elevator that we took to the second floor. Our first room was just two down from the elevator: 211. I set down the luggage and opened the door, turning on the lights. "Here you go. Get some rest."

"Where are you staying?" she asked groggily.

"I'm just next door."

"We could have shared a room," she said, almost slurring her words. "Saved money."

"It's okay," I said. I led her inside the room. There were two queen beds. I helped her over to the far bed, then knelt down and took off her shoes.

She smiled. "You're really nice. Have I told you you're really nice?"

"You just did," I said. I pulled down the sheets on her bed. "There you go."

"I wish you could stay."

I grinned. "It's a good thing you don't drink," I said. "Good night." I leaned forward and kissed her forehead. She wrapped her arms around me. "Thank you." She kissed my cheek, then lingered, her arms still around me.

"C'mon, sweetie," I said. "It's time for bed." I put my hands on her arms and lightly pushed back. "Now go back to sleep."

She giggled. "I need to brush my teeth."

"Your suitcase is right here. I'm just next door. Call me when you wake in the morning. Good night."

"Good night, handsome."

"Good night." As I stepped out of her room, I hoped that she wouldn't remember anything she'd said. From what I knew of her I was certain she'd be embarrassed and feel guilty. I went into my own room, took off my shoes, and fell back onto the bed. I fell asleep with my clothes on, on top of the covers.

CHAPTER

Seventeen

July 9, 1986

Dear Diary,

My body is changing. I have what they call the pregnancy mask, though it really just looks like I need to wash my face. The skin is also darkening around my nipples and belly button. Mrs. Churcher is keeping me very busy helping her clean the house and watch the boys. Fortunately it's not a big house, and I like the boys. Charles is very bright. He asks me questions about my pregnancy, some not appropriate. I don't tell his mother. Mrs. Churcher leaves the house a lot with her friends. Mr. Churcher is very kind. I'm anxious around men right now. I've been abandoned by all the men in my life. I feel like Fantine in Les Misérables. But I must admit that Mr. Churcher is nicer to me than the women in my life.

Noel

DECEMBER 17

I had a bizarre dream again. One I remembered and woke hoping wasn't real. Or a harbinger of things to come. It was of my dream girl again, only this time every time I reached out to her, my father stood in front of her, blocking my view of her. She was reaching out to me.

I woke the next morning to the sun streaming into my room. It took me a moment to realize where I was. I sat up, rubbed my eyes, and yawned, then stood and walked over to the window. Even though we were in Arizona, there was still snow on the ground. Flagstaff is one of the only large cities in Arizona that has four seasons.

I knew this about Flagstaff as I had once done research on the city. One of my characters was driving Route 66. The famous road passes directly through Flagstaff, which not only averages a hundred inches of snow a year but is also the highest point on the route.

I looked over at the clock. It was almost nine. I wasn't surprised that I'd slept so late. I had gotten up the day before at five a.m. and not gone to bed until one forty a.m. Just then my cell phone rang. It was Laurie. I sat up in bed and answered.

"Are you home?"

"No. I'm in Arizona."

Long pause. "What are you doing in Arizona?"

"Warming up."

"You could just put on a sweater for that. You drove, no doubt."

"Of course I did."

"May I ask why you're in Arizona?"

"I'm looking for my father."

She let out a soft sigh. "And when were you going to tell me this?"

"When I got around to it," I said.

"You are such a pain."

"I do my best. And that's why my books sell. It's all that pain I share. It's schadenfreude."

"Schadenfreude," she echoed. I could envision her rolling her eyes.

"I need you to do something for me," I said.

"Name it."

"I need you to book a couple of rooms at the Phoenician."

"This close to Christmas, you know they're going to be sold out."

"I know. That's why I'm asking you to do it. You can work magic."

She groaned. "The things I do for you."

"That's why I love you. Let me know when you've got it."

She groaned. "Ciao."

"Bye." I hung up, then dialed Rachel's room. She answered on the first ring.

"There you are," she said brightly.

"You were supposed to call me."

"I know. I didn't want to wake you. You needed the sleep. How long have you been up?"

"I just woke up," I said. "How about you?"

"I've been up about an hour. I've been getting ready."

"I still need to shower. I'll be ready in a half hour. I'll knock on your door when I'm done."

"See you then."

I showered and dressed, wearing lighter clothes than the day before. It wouldn't be short-sleeve weather, but compared to Utah, it was a heat wave. As I walked out my door, Rachel emerged from her room pulling her bag.

"Good morning," I said.

"Hi," she said softly, parting her hair from her face. "They have a complimentary breakfast downstairs."

"Good. I need a coffee. Or two."

I grabbed her bag and we took the stairs down to the main floor. The dining area was in a small room at the side of the lobby. I got some scrambled egg concoction with parsley flakes, croutons, and Swiss cheese, while Rachel got a bowl of oatmeal and English muffins, which she spread thickly with orange marmalade. With the exception of an old man watching CNN, we were the only ones in the dining room.

After we started eating, Rachel said, "What time did we get here last night?"

"It was a little after one thirty."

"Oh," she said. She hesitated, then went back to eating her oatmeal.

I watched her spoon a few bites, then asked, "Are you okay?"

She looked up anxiously. "Did I embarrass myself last night?"

"No."

"I don't believe you."

"You were a little . . . affectionate."

She groaned. "I'm so sorry. I get crazy at night."

"Best time to get crazy," I said.

"I've always been that way. When I get really sleepy, it's like I turn into a completely different person; half the time I don't even remember what I say. Please don't tell anyone."

I cocked my head. "Who exactly would I tell? Oh, wait. I could call your fiancé."

"That would not go over well."

"Or I could just put it in a book."

"You wouldn't dare."

"You have no idea what I would dare."

She looked at me like she wasn't sure if I was being serious or not. "You wouldn't, would you?"

"No. That's the best way to get sued." I changed the subject. "So, I had a freaky dream last night. It was your mother again, only this time my father stood in front of her, like he was trying to shield her from me."

"You don't think he would try to keep us from her."

"I have no idea."

"My mother aside, you must have a lot of things you want to talk to him about."

"The only thing I want to know is why he abandoned me in an abusive home and never came back."

"Maybe he was abusive too."

I took a sip of my coffee. "Maybe. I don't have any recollection of that. But maybe. Neglect is abuse too." I suddenly smiled darkly. "Maybe it's like 'A Boy Named Sue.'"

Rachel looked at me quizzically. "What's that?"

"Really, you've never heard of it?"

She shook her head.

"It's an old Johnny Cash song. A father names his boy Sue before leaving him with nothing. Going through life with a girl's name makes him learn how to fight and defend himself. When he's older he decides that when he finds his father, he's going to kill him. Instead, the father tells him that he knew he wasn't going to be around, so he gave him that name to make him tough."

"That doesn't make sense. He gave him a girl's name to make him tough?"

"Yeah. So when he finds his father, they have a big fight and the son finally wins and he's about to kill his father when his father says something like, 'You ought to thank me, before I die, For the gravel in your guts and the spit in your eye.'"

"Why didn't he just change his name?"

I grinned. "Then there wouldn't be a song."

She took a bite of her muffin, then said, "Why do we always take the hard way?"

My phone vibrated. I looked down. Laurie had texted me.

> Could only get one room—a suite with two beds. Under your name. You owe me big time, Mr. Big Time author. ☺

I looked back up.

"Who's that?"

"My agent. I asked her to book us some rooms."

"Really? She'll do that for you?"

"She does whatever it takes."

"Whatever it takes to do what?"

"To keep me happy."

"That must be nice."

I looked at my watch. "It's about ten thirty. If we leave now, that would put us in Scottsdale around one."

"Scottsdale?"

"Laurie booked us rooms at the Phoenician Resort. Actually, she booked us one room. A suite. She had to pull strings to get it. Are you okay with sharing a room, or should we try to find something else?"

"It's okay," she said. "I trust you."

I grinned. "After last night, the real question is, Do I trust you?"

She rubbed her forehead. "I'm so embarrassed. Please let me live this down."

I laughed. "I won't bring it up again."

"Thank you."

"So, we check into the hotel, have lunch. That would put us at around three."

"How far is Mesa from Scottsdale?"

"It's only about twenty minutes. I think I'd rather wait until evening to drop by, so we have a little time to kill."

"We could stop in Sedona," Rachel said. "It's only an

hour from here. I've always wanted to see it. And they say it has good energy. It's the vortexes or something."

"I could use good energy."

"Like your energy shots?"

"I'll take it however I can get it."

CHAPTER *Eighteen*

July 16, 1986

Dear Diary,

Today Jacob called me Mommy. I know little kids sometimes accidentally call their teachers Mommy, so it's no big deal. Unfortunately it was in front of Mrs. Churcher. She wasn't very happy about that. Life goes on. I keep getting bigger. Next week, my friend Diane is going to drive down from Logan to see me. I'm lonely. It's strange to say that when there's another human inside me. I wonder what he or she is like. I wonder if we'll be friends someday. I wonder if she'll ever forgive me.

Noel

I checked us out of the hotel, carried both of our bags out to the car, and we drove out of town. In Flagstaff the freeway changed from Interstate 89 to Interstate 17 and we continued south, dropping in altitude as well as latitude.

After a few miles of comfortable silence Rachel turned to me. "Is it hard writing romances?"

"I don't really write romances. I write love stories."

"What's the difference?"

"Love stories are more universal."

"What does that mean?"

"They're about more than boy meets girl. The stories have universal themes that everyone can relate to."

"Everyone can relate to romance."

I looked at her. "Can they?"

She bit her lip. "Maybe not."

"Also, in a love story, the endings vary. Did you see the movie *Titanic*?"

"Yes."

"Love story. Rose falls in love with Jack, the standard rich girl/poor boy scenario, but in the end, the boat sinks and Jack drowns."

"Yeah, that kind of sucked."

I laughed. "Romances are more formulaic. Boy meets girl, boy loses girl, boy and girl end up together. Think Cinderella. The prince dances with Cinderella at the ball, Cinderella runs off at midnight, the prince tracks down Cinderella with the glass slipper she left behind. Cinderella ditches her ugly stepsisters, and she and the prince live happily ever after."

"Do they always live happily ever after?"

"They do in the romance genre. In love stories, it depends."

"On what?"

I grinned. "Whether or not there's a sequel."

When we passed the first sign for Sedona, Rachel said, "Have you heard that song 'There Is No Arizona'?"

"Who sings it?"

"Jamie O'Neal."

"Don't know her."

"Really? You've never heard it?"

"Don't give me grief. You've never heard of 'A Boy Named Sue,' and Johnny Cash is definitely more famous than this O'Neal woman." I looked over. "So, what's it about?"

"It's about a woman whose man goes to Arizona and tells her that he'll send for her after he gets things in order. He keeps sending her postcards, but he was really just lying about the whole thing. In the end she concludes that there's no Arizona."

"Hence the title. That's tragic."

"Very. Definitely not a romance."

"Not much of a love story either," I said. I glanced over. "Why did you think of that?"

"The chorus goes, 'There is no Arizona, no painted desert, no Sedona.'"

"Ms. O'Neal was wrong," I said. "I just saw a sign."

By the time we reached Sedona, there was no trace of winter. Ahead of us, jagged red sandstone formations jutted up from the stubbled Sonoran Desert plains.

Our entire side trip lasted less than four hours. We drove downtown and walked through the Main Street District full of sidewalk cafés, art galleries, jewelry stores, and tourist shops selling T-shirts and Sedona memorabilia.

After that we drove up to the chapel of the Holy Cross,

which looked out over the valley. Most of the people inside the church were foreigners. In spite of Sedona's reputation as a New Age mecca, it is actually a religious town and there are myriad churches scattered around the natural rock cathedrals.

We could have easily spent more time sightseeing, but I was beginning to feel like I was avoiding something, which, no doubt, I was. I'm a savant at finding distractions when something's uncomfortable. It's amazing how many distractions arise when I'm not in the mood to write.

We finally headed back to I-17 and drove the remaining couple of hours to Scottsdale. The temperature in Phoenix was pleasant, hovering in the low seventies. Rachel was glad for the warmth, as she wasn't as used to the cold as I was. St. George, which is near her home, is among the warmest parts of Utah and never really gets very cold. It's the place where Salt Lakers go to golf in the winter or escape the gray-brown air of Salt Lake's frequent inversions.

The Phoenician is a green napkin on the dusty stone lap of Camelback Mountain. As we drove down the immaculate palm-tree-lined streets and well-groomed greens of the resort, Rachel looked around in wonder. "This is really nice," she said. "It must cost a fortune to stay here."

"It's not cheap," I said. "Especially this time of the year."

"We could have stayed somewhere less expensive."

"We could have, but I'm still trying to impress you."

She smiled. "It's still working."

We drove past the hotel's main entrance to the upper property—the luxury Canyon Suites. I suppose that I was showing off a little. Or a lot. Two young men wearing matching uniforms of hunter-green shorts, caps, and smock-like blouses met us beneath the portico. One of them took my car while the other put our luggage on a cart and wheeled it inside.

Rachel and I went inside the beautiful, marble-floored lobby and checked in at a desk with an attractive older woman. As the woman handed us our room keys, she said, "Welcome to the Canyons, Mr. Churcher. Forgive me for gushing, but I'm a big fan of your work. I hope you and Mrs. Churcher enjoy your stay with us. If there's anything I can do to make your stay more pleasant, please don't hesitate to call me."

I was about to correct her on our matrimonial state, but Rachel spoke first. "Thank you, Claire. We're looking forward to our honeymoon."

"Forgive me," she replied. "I wasn't told that it was your honeymoon. Congratulations. I'll have a bottle of champagne sent to your room."

"Thank you," I said, standing.

As we walked away from the desk, I said, "Our honeymoon?"

Rachel smiled. "Just protecting your reputation, Mr. Churcher. Don't want your fans to get the wrong impression."

I nodded. "That was thoughtful of you. And we got a bottle of champagne out of it."

We followed the bellboy with our luggage rack down the soft carpeted corridor about a hundred feet to our room. I unlocked the door and the bellboy brought in our suitcases.

The suite was spacious and beautiful, and as Rachel walked in, her eyes grew wide with wonder. She walked over to a double glass door that led to a wide patio that overlooked the golf course. Outside our window was a colorful cactus garden. "What a view." She walked around the rest of the suite, disappearing into another room. After the bellboy left, I turned up the air-conditioning. "What do you think?"

Rachel walked back into the room. "So this is how the other two percent live."

I sat back on the couch. "I could still try to book us something on Airbnb."

"No, I'm good," she said. "This room is really, really big."

"It's eighteen hundred square feet. It's bigger than my mother's house. Of course, I usually just get the one bedroom."

"Then you've been here before?"

"Many times. Phoenix has some classic bookstores I come to for book signings. There's the Changing Hands Bookstore in Tempe and The Poisoned Pen in Scottsdale."

"What an amazing life you have," she said.

"An amazingly lonely one," I replied. "Once I came here

in the dead of summer. It was a hundred and seventeen degrees."

"That sounds awful."

"At first I thought the same thing. But actually it turned out quite nice. Hardly anyone was here and I pretty much had the pool and service to myself. Speaking of which, I was thinking we should have lunch by the pool."

"Should I put on my swimsuit?"

"If you want to swim."

"I'll be right back."

A few minutes later she returned in a bright-red halter-top tankini. She had a beautiful figure, which she modestly covered. She looked at me as if awaiting my approval. I was speechless.

"So? Do you like it?"

"Wow."

"Wow?"

"It's beautiful." I looked into her eyes. "You're beautiful."

She looked at me doubtfully, then down at her suit. "It's not too . . . risqué?"

"Maybe for the nineteen hundreds," I said.

"I'm sorry, I'm just self-conscious."

"With a body like yours, most of the women I've dated would wear as little as they could get away with."

"Well, that wouldn't be me." She glanced at herself in the mirror. "It's the suit. It's flattering."

"That's like saying the *Mona Lisa* has a nice frame."

She laughed. "Stop it." She looked at me and said, "Brandon thinks it's too immodest."

"That suit?"

She nodded. "I wore it once, then put it away. Sometimes I think he'd have me wear a burka if he could."

"That would be putting a candle under a bushel," I said.

She laughed again. "Are you putting on your suit?"

"Ugh," I said. I wasn't dying to expose my physique. "Yes. But I'm warning you, I have an author's body."

"You have a nice body."

"Now you've really lost all credibility. Give me a moment."

I went into the bathroom and slipped into my black Tommy Bahamas swimsuit and a Green Day T-shirt, then came back out.

"All right. Let's go."

The Canyon had its own palm-tree-lined pool surrounded by luxurious wooden lounge chairs and amber-colored cabanas. There were several dozen people outside but no children, so the pool area was quiet. We sat down at a table near the pool and a server approached us.

"Good afternoon. Will you be dining?"

"Yes," I said.

He handed us lunch menus. "Can I get you something to drink?"

"I'll have a Diet Coke with lime, and she would like . . ." I glanced over at Rachel.

She looked up at the server. "I'd like a pineapple juice with a splash of cranberry juice."

"With vodka?"

She looked surprised by the question. "No, sir."

"One virgin sea breeze and a Diet Coke."

He returned a few moments later with our drinks and took our orders. I ordered a Mediterranean chicken wrap. Rachel ordered the chicken and kale Caesar salad.

As we ate, we talked about the resort and Arizona's climate, comparing it to Rachel's home in St. George. It was tempting to avoid thinking about the reason we'd come to Phoenix. Especially since every time I did, I was filled with anxiety.

Had I been too rash in coming? Was I only here for Rachel? I had no idea how my father would respond to the meeting. I wasn't even sure how I'd respond. Elyse had said that he wanted to see me, but why? Was he regretful and trying to make amends? Or was this one of those cliché cases where the parent returns after their child makes it big? What if he asked me for money? Or a kidney? You can see why I didn't want to think about it.

Peculiarly, Rachel didn't bring it up either, though I think she might have sensed my reticence and was waiting for me to broach the subject. After a while she went for a swim, first dipping her feet into the water, then sliding in off the edge. The pool was about four feet deep, shallow enough for her to stand and talk to me.

"This is perfect. Come in."

I smiled at her. "I'm good."

"I know you're good. Come in."

"I can't. I just ate. You shouldn't swim for at least a half hour after you eat."

"That's a myth. If you cramp up, I'll save you. I promise."

I grinned. "All right. I've run out of excuses. But don't look as I take off my shirt. The glare might blind you."

"I have been warned," she said.

I took off my shirt and got in the pool. She was right, the water did feel great. Rachel leaned back against the side of the pool, resting her arms on the cement ledge. "Do you remember what we were talking about this morning, at breakfast?"

"You mean . . ." I hesitated bringing it up. "How you were acting last night."

She frowned. "You said you wouldn't bring that up again."

"I didn't. I thought you were."

"I won't ever bring that up."

"All right, so what were we talking about?"

"We were talking about that 'Boy Named Sue' song. And I asked 'Why do we always take the hard way?'"

"I remember."

"I've been thinking about that. And I think I figured out why. It's because we don't believe that we're worthy of happiness. Or love." She looked me in the eyes, then said, "At least, that's what I was thinking."

"I understand that," I said. "I've always believed that we don't choose the life we want. We choose the life we think we deserve. We self-sabotage as a way to punish ourselves."

"Why would we punish ourselves?" Rachel asked. "Doesn't the world punish us enough?"

I frowned. "Why wouldn't we? We live in a world that's always making us work for love. It's cause and effect. That's the story of my childhood. If I can be good enough, maybe my mother will love me.

"The problem is, somewhere along the way you figure out that you can't ever be good enough. It finally just got to be too much for me. You hit this point where you just want to scream, 'Love me for who I am or get out of my life.'

"I think that's why I was never interested in religion. Everyone I talked to about religion basically said I'd have to work really hard to earn God's love. I spent half my life working just to get my mother's love and it didn't work.

"Some would give me this explanation that we were really just finding our way back to God. The way I see it, it's like this: Would you take a kid, drop him off in the middle of China, then say, 'I'm going to disappear now. It's your job to find your way back to me. There will be thousands of people giving you different directions and different maps and you'll never really know if the one you choose is right. But if you screw up, you can't come back home.' I know what it is to be kicked out of your home by the ones you love and not know why. If that's God, an omnipotent version of my mother, I want no part of him."

Rachel looked at me thoughtfully. "I told you that my parents were really strict. They're highly legalistic in their approach to God. In their minds, God is like a cosmic traffic cop. For every action there must be an equal and opposite reaction. If you make a mistake, you must be punished. Which is why they've always been highly punitive. I can't tell you how many times they beat me. What made it worse is they would express their love to me as they did it. It was pretty messed up."

"Your parents beat you?"

"Frequently. And with holy intent, sometimes even quoting the Bible as they did. Proverbs thirteen twenty-four: 'He who withholds his rod hates his son.' Proverbs twenty-three fourteen: 'Thou shalt beat him with the rod, and shalt deliver his soul from Sheol.' They got it all in writing."

"I'm sorry."

"Yeah. Me too. But the thing is, I think Proverbs was just King Solomon's parenting style. And wise or not, his son, Rehoboam, who took his place, was a vicious, cruel leader whom everyone hated and was almost killed by his own people. So what Solomon indirectly was saying was, 'My parenting advice stinks, and if you want a kid like mine, raise him the way I did.'"

I laughed. "How do you know so much about the Bible?"

"My family studied the Bible every day before school."

"I'm impressed."

"Don't be," she said. "They made me. So at first I just accepted their twist on everything. Then, as I got older, I realized that they were adding their own interpretations and personalities to their teachings, so I started studying not to please them but to figure out the truth of what was written in the Bible. I started asking questions."

"How did that go?"

"They saw it as rebellion. Like most people, they were more interested in protecting their beliefs than learning the truth. I kept seeing these contradictions in what I read and what they believed. When I was sixteen I asked them what grace meant, and my father said, 'Grace means that after you do everything you can possibly do, then, and only then, is God's grace sufficient to save you.' I walked away despairing. I thought, That's impossible. No one can do *all* they can do. Because you can always pray for one more second or give one more dollar to the poor or read one more word in the Bible. You can always do more. And everyone screws up sometime and that alone means you haven't done all you could have done."

She breathed out in exasperation. "I've seen people spend their entire lives chasing their spiritual tails and end up nothing but exhausted. People who believe in a traffic-cop God end up either full of shame or full of delusional self-righteousness. I think that sums up my parents. Both of those things. If you were to ask them if they were good, they would say no. But if you were to ask them if they were sinners, they would be offended.

"The hard part is that even though you know it's not right, once that mind-set is programmed into you, good luck getting it out. Because it feels like you are constantly rebelling against what's right even if you know it's not right." She squinted at me. "Am I making any sense?"

I nodded. "More than I've heard in a long time," I said.

"And you're making an absentee father sound better and better."

"It's not better. It's just different. It's like saying which is better, abuse or neglect. Like you said, they're both forms of abuse. It's just that one is passive."

I thought over her comment, then looked down at my watch. "Speaking of neglect, it's past five. We better go."

We climbed out of the pool, dried ourselves off, and walked back to our suite. I changed back into my clothes in the bathroom while Rachel did the same in the master bedroom.

Preparing to see my father, I had one of those "first day at school" moments where I wondered what I should wear. I told myself that it didn't matter and put on a T-shirt and khaki shorts and tennis shoes with no socks and went out to get my car. If he didn't want to see me in a T-shirt, why would he want to see me in an Armani jacket?

The valet brought up my car and handed me the keys. "Have a good evening."

"Thank you."

I had already opened the door for Rachel, and she climbed in next to me.

"Are you ready?" she asked.

"No. Are you?"

"Nope. Let's go."

I smiled. I loved this woman's spirit.

CHAPTER *Nineteen*

July 23, 1986

Dear Diary,

Tomorrow is the 24th—that's Pioneer Day here in Utah. We're all going to the Salt Lake County Fair and a rodeo. I'm very excited about that. I haven't been out much. We have rodeos up in Logan. They're always fun to watch. My stomach just keeps growing. I have some pain down my leg. Mrs. Churcher says that it's my sciatic nerve and is no big deal. It will go away. I'm glad for that. Having a baby is a big commitment. Not something you think about when some boy is taking your clothes off. I wonder if I'll ever see Peter again or what I'll say to him if I do. It will probably never happen. That's okay—I have a boyfriend. His name is Jacob, and he loves me more than any boy has ever loved a girl. He told me so.

Noel

I programmed my father's address into my phone and Rachel and I set off.

The drive from Scottsdale to Mesa took us only twenty-five minutes. Fortunately it was a Saturday; otherwise we would have hit rush-hour traffic. We drove south on the 101 to US 60, where we drove east to the South Gilbert Road exit, then north on Gilbert to Broadway. There we turned east, driving a short distance to Twenty-Fifth Street and then south a block to Calypso Avenue and my father's neighborhood.

It was a simple, middle-class suburb with smallish homes. I found the address painted in black and white on the curb. Number 2412.

The home was one of the older ones—a bland, chiffon-yellow stucco rambler with a two-car garage and a terra-cotta tiled roof. The front yard was austere, landscaped all in red lava rock with a small cactus garden in the center. Near the home's front door was a large clay pot with a small lemon tree, which looked slightly at odds with the Christmas wreath hanging on the door. I pulled the car up to the curb.

"That's the place," I said.

"It looks nice," Rachel said. "Simple."

I glanced over at her. "What do you think? Ready to meet this guy?"

"I don't think I should go with you. I will if you want me to, but it's a big moment. Me being there might just confuse things."

I thought for a moment, then said, "You're probably right. If things go well, I'll come get you."

"Good luck," she said. "I'll say a prayer for you."

I got out of the car and walked up to the door, looking

for any sign of life. There was a folded copy of the *Arizona Republic* newspaper on the front porch near the door.

I rang the doorbell and a dog inside the house started barking. A small dog with a yappy bark.

I heard footsteps and the door opened. A woman, tall and thin with slightly graying hair, opened the door. She had kind eyes.

"May I help you?" she asked gently.

"I'm here to see Scott Churcher."

"Scott's not here right now. May I help you?"

"Do you know when he'll be back?"

She looked at me for a moment, then said, "You're Jacob."

I looked at her quizzically. "How did you know?"

"You look like Scott. Will you come in?"

"Thank you, but I have someone in the car. When do you expect him?"

"He's in Tucson today, but he'll be back tomorrow afternoon. Is that all right?"

"That's fine," I said.

"I'll let him know that you came by. What time should I tell him you'll be here?"

"What time do you expect him back?"

"Three. But if he knows you're here, he'll be back earlier."

"Three is fine," I said. "I'll come back then."

"Would you like to leave your phone number?"

"No."

"All right," she said kindly. "We'll see you tomorrow."

As I started to turn, she said, "Jacob."

I turned back. "Yes?"

"Thank you for coming by. He'll be very happy to see you."

I nodded slightly, then went back to the car.

CHAPTER

Twenty

July 30, 1986

Dear Diary,

I didn't get to go to the rodeo. It wasn't the Churchers' fault. My father called and asked if they were going anywhere for the 24th. When Scott told him we were going to the rodeo, my dad said I must not go, since they knew a lot of people were going there from Logan. I don't think my parents really care about me. All they care about is how they look to the neighbors they go to church with. I once read this in the Bible—something like, they are like sepulchres, white and shiny on the outside but filled with dead men's bones. That's my parents, all right. Their life is a lie. I would rather live an honest life than an admired lie. Besides, no one ever is really happy for people who are having only good things happen. They resent them because behind their own masks they are hurting too.

I spend a lot of time snuggling with little Jacob. He's my buddy. I love Charles too, but he's not close to me the way Jacob is. He used to like it when I read to him, but now he just reads to himself. I think he resents me because he wants his mother, and since I came she hasn't given the boys much attention. I think maybe she was tired before and is now enjoying her freedom. My mother sent me a letter. I haven't opened it.

Noel

I climbed back into the car. Rachel looked at me with anticipation. "Was he there?"

"No. He's in Tucson. He gets back tomorrow afternoon."

"Are we coming back?"

I started the car. "Yes." I pulled away from the curb, eager to leave the house. I didn't speak, and about five minutes later Rachel asked, "Are you okay?"

I just looked ahead. "I don't know."

"Are we going back to the hotel?"

I glanced over at her. "Yes. Unless there's someplace else you'd like to go."

"No. Would you like to go for a walk when we get back?"

I didn't answer immediately. "We'll see."

Twenty minutes later we pulled into the resort. The valet opened the door for Rachel as I got out. I handed him the keys.

"It's such a nice night," Rachel said. "How about that walk?"

"Are you trying to keep me busy?"

"Yes."

"Okay." I turned to the valet, who was just about to get in my car. "Where's a good place to hike?"

"There's a good trail to Camelback, but you're a little too late for that for tonight. This trail right here leads around the property and past the cactus garden. It's a nice walk."

"Thank you," I said.

"If you do Camelback, be sure to take a lot of water with you."

"Thank you."

We walked up on the trail, which led us down to the main resort. The path was beautiful and along it were myriad species of cacti and large magenta hedges of bougainvillea. The foliage was pretty but most of it was prickly, which reminded me of many of the women I had dated recently.

Rachel was a little quiet, no doubt because I was. We walked about fifty yards in silence before she asked again, "Are you okay?"

I looked down. "I'm not sure what I am. I'm sorry, I guess I'm spinning out a little."

"It's okay. I can't imagine how hard this must be."

We kept walking. We were near the golf course when Rachel's phone rang. "I'm sorry, I forgot to turn it off." She looked at the screen, then answered it. "Hi."

A male voice began shouting. I couldn't make out the words, just the angry, nasal tone of the assault.

"I'm sorry, I . . ." Shouting. "I forgot . . . I'm sorry . . ." Shouting. "I'm really sorry." More shouting. Her eyes began to well up. "I know. I'm sorry. Please forgive me." Another burst. "I—I—" Gasp. "I'm sorry, he wasn't there. I'm sorry." The voice settled some. "Okay. I'll try. Call me later. I love you too. Bye."

She hung up the phone, then turned away from me. "Are you okay?" I asked.

"I'm sorry . . ."

"You don't need to say you're sorry to me."

"I'm sorry." She shook her head. It was like she had been so conditioned to apologize for herself that she couldn't do otherwise.

"Do you know how many times you just told him you were sorry?"

She suddenly looked angry. "Why? Were you counting?"

I just looked at her. "I wasn't insulting you. I just wanted to point out . . ." I sighed. "Is that how he always talks to you?"

She didn't answer.

"It's not respectful. It's not a healthy way to have a relationship."

"You're giving me relationship advice now? How's all that wisdom working for you?"

Her words stung. I just looked at her, momentarily dumbstruck. Then I breathed out. "Sorry. It's none of my business." I turned to walk away.

I had taken a dozen steps when she called after me. "Jacob."

I turned back. She walked up to me.

There were tears in her eyes. "I'm sorry." She put her arms around me. "Please forgive me. I didn't mean that. I'm just upset."

After a moment I said, "All right. Let's go back to the hotel."

She wiped her eyes. "I need some time alone."

I looked at her, then nodded. "I'll be back in the room." I reached in my pocket and brought out a plastic keycard. "Here's the key. Be safe." I leaned forward and kissed her on the forehead. Then I turned and walked back down the path toward the hotel.

I was still hurting when I got back to the suite. What she said had pierced. The truth always hurts, right? But my pain wasn't just from her attack. I was angry at Rachel's fiancé. And I was angry at her for allowing herself to be treated so poorly.

As I thought it over, I realized I was also angry at myself. I was angry because I was falling for her. I was falling for a woman who was engaged to another man. No, I wasn't falling. I *had* fallen. I had already hit the water. I was drenched.

And to make it worse, she was with someone who I didn't think deserved her. Not that I really knew that; I'd never met him and no doubt my judgment, as a matter of self-interest, would be skewed. But I knew for certain that

I never would have talked to her the way he just had. The more I thought about it, the more I realized that I needed to tell her how I felt.

I got a mini bottle of Jack Daniel's out of the refrigerator, poured it into a glass with a Coke and ice, and took a drink. After a few sips my thoughts changed. *What was I thinking?* This woman was getting married. She had already ordered the flowers and booked the reception center. I had only known her for a few days. I ran a great risk in telling her. She would shut me out. No, it was better to just follow the plan.

I grabbed the remote, then sat back in an armchair and turned on the television. The Arizona Cardinals were playing the Denver Broncos. I watched for a few minutes, not that I cared about either team; I really just needed a distraction while I drank.

After a second drink, I remembered Noel's diary. Rachel had left it on the nightstand next to her bed. I picked it up, then turned off the television and took off my shoes and lay across my bed.

August 6, 1986

Dear Diary,

Something horrible beyond words happened. While I was at the doctor's, Charles climbed a tree and grabbed on to a power line. He was electrocuted. Little Jacob was with him. He ran back home and got his mother. When I got home the ambulance was still at the house, but no one was moving quickly. When I got close I saw his little body covered by the sheet. I confess, my first fear was that it was my little Jacob. I felt guilty about that. I don't know what will happen with me. Maybe they will send me to another home. Not my home. That would never happen. I still haven't read the letter from my mother. I don't know if I ever will. There is so much pain in this world.

Noel

✦

August 13, 1986

Dear Diary,

I am halfway through my pregnancy. It's hard to even think of me or my baby at this time. Charles's funeral was last Thursday. It was the saddest thing I've ever seen. When they shut the lid on the coffin, Mrs. Churcher fell on the ground and wailed. I worry for her. She has not stopped crying. She doesn't eat. She stays in her bed all day with the light out. She has told me at least five times that she wants to die. One time she asked me to bring her sleeping pills. When I came in she yelled at me because she wanted the whole bottle. I just left her room. I knew she wouldn't come out. She never comes out.

Noel

August 20, 1986

Dear Diary,

Things here are not getting worse or better. The world is stuck in a hopeless limbo. There is a darkness that pervades everything. Through it all, it's as if they've forgotten that they still have a son. My poor little Jacob. He clings to me all the time now. I hold him. He kisses me at night when I put him to bed. I am all he has, mostly. Mr. and Mrs. Churcher got into a big fight. I heard something break. Mr. Churcher came out of the room. He looked at me, and I could see his pain.

I finally opened the letter my mother wrote me. I wish I hadn't. She told me that I was such a disappointment to the family, and that she has racked her brain trying to figure out where she had gone wrong. Then God told her the truth. She hadn't gone wrong—I had. She was relieved of her guilt and is now worried about my soul. She said I was a chewed piece of gum and no one would want me. I wish she would worry less about my soul and more about me. Or even the baby she pretends doesn't exist. I wish I had never opened the letter. I wish I had never been born. Then I wouldn't be the cause of so much trouble.

Noel

August 27, 1986

Dear Diary,

I am having a little girl. A sweet little girl. It's hard for me not to name her. Before I came here, my father told me not to name my baby. He said it would make it much harder when I gave my baby up. Then he told me that when he was little he lived on a farm and they raised pigs. He named one of the pigs Wilbur after the pig in Charlotte's Web. Then they slaughtered Wilbur for Christmas dinner. He said it was his worst Christmas ever. I think that was the worst story ever. Did he really compare my baby to a pig?

I'm not going to name her.

Noel

It was dark outside when I heard the doorknob turn and the door open. I looked at my watch. It was a quarter past nine. I walked out to the foyer. Rachel was letting herself in, trying to be quiet about it.

"Hi."

She turned to me. "Oh, hi. I thought you might be in bed already."

"No. I'm a night owl."

She walked up to me. "I'm so ashamed about what I said to you. I don't know where that came from. I'm just such an emotional mess. I'm getting married in four months. I shouldn't have come. It was selfish of me."

I looked at her, disappointed in the conclusion she'd arrived at. "Taking care of yourself isn't selfish. Especially when others aren't."

She forced a smile, though her eyes still looked dull and puffy. "It's been a long day. I'm going to take a shower and go to bed. Thank you for this lovely room." She kissed me on the cheek. "Good night." Then she walked into her room and shut and locked her door, leaving my heart and mind still reeling. Mostly my heart.

My heart hurt. I was in love. And I was stupid to let my guard down. *When had my feelings crossed that line?* I went to my room and lay back on the bed. Laurie was right. I never should have stirred the ashes.

CHAPTER Twenty-One

September 3, 1986

Dear Diary,

I know I wrote that I wouldn't give my baby a name, but I can't help it. I know that it won't even keep. I'm calling her Angela. Like an angel. That's what she is. And if she's born on Christmas like I was, she'll be a Christmas Angel. This was a pretty good week. Nothing big or important happened. Maybe that's why it was a good week. The weather is getting colder. No matter the weather, I think this is going to be a long, long winter.

Noel

✦

September 17, 1986

Dear Diary,

Looking through a National Geographic magazine at the doctor's office, I saw a picture of a boa constrictor that had swallowed a pig whole, and I thought, That looks just like me. Well, without the scales and fangs. I'm huge. Someone in the doctor's office asked me if my husband wanted a boy or a girl. I told her that he was fine with either. I feel so alone. I'm so tempted to reach out to Peter, but I won't. I've made enough mistakes in my life. If he loves me, he'll come back to me. If he doesn't love me, why would I want him to?

Noel

DECEMBER 18

I woke early the next morning. Rachel was still sleeping, so I wrote her a note, then put on my bathing suit and went out to the pool. I was still hurting from the night before. I was seething with jealousy and there was no reason for me to believe that she would leave him. Part of me didn't even want to see her.

There were only a handful of guests in the pool area and only one other person actually in the pool.

I jumped in and started swimming laps. About a half hour later I noticed that Rachel had come out. She waved at me. I swam over to the side of the pool. She looked like she felt better than she had the night before. She looked lighter.

"Don't wear yourself out," she said, crouching down near the edge of the pool. "I was thinking, since we have the time, maybe we should hike Camelback. Want to? The concierge says it takes about two hours each way. She gave me a map."

"I'm game," I said. I got out and went back to the room

and got dressed. As I walked out of the bathroom, Rachel was sitting on the couch.

"How are you feeling today?" I asked.

She looked at me with soft eyes. "I still feel bad about my behavior last night. You've been nothing but good to me." She shook her head. "It was the guilt. And I took it out on you."

"We don't need to talk about it," I said. "I understand."

She smiled a half smile. "At least one of us does."

I took her hand to pull her up from the couch. "Let's go climb the mountain." I lifted her.

After she was standing, she still clung to my hand. She smiled awkwardly, then let go. "Sorry."

We stopped at a sundries shop in the resort for lip balm, sunscreen, and water. I bought myself a hat and Rachel a bandana, which I helped her wrap around her head. She looked really cute.

We parked near the base of the mountain and took the Cholla Trail to the summit. The trail was well marked and the landscape was rugged and beautiful with saguaro cacti popping up around the mountain.

We made it to the craggy summit in a little more than an hour and a half. We had a 365-degree view of Phoenix, a checkered grid of dusty green flora, red tile roofs, and blue swimming pools. From this vantage, Phoenix looked like anything but Christmas. There was a nice, steady breeze, and I sat down on a flat, wide rock to take it in.

There were others on the summit, at least a dozen or more hikers, and they were generous with their water.

One man had carried a dozen bottles up just to hand out along the way. He told me that just two months earlier a man from France had died of sunstroke near the summit. He hadn't thought to bring any water with him.

Rachel walked around the summit and, not surprisingly, several men flirted with her. She was laughing with them, innocently, but it still felt like little pinpricks on my heart. I kept waiting for her to come sit by me but she never did. Finally I got up. "We better go back down."

"Wait," she said, walking over. "I want to get a picture of us."

She beckoned one of the flirting men over to take her phone. Clearly a body builder, he was wearing a tank top that exposed muscular arms the size of my thighs. He switched her phone to take a selfie. "Sorry," he said. "Got a picture of me. You can keep it, no charge."

Rachel slid up next to me on the rock. "Okay, do it right this time," she said. Even though she had apologized about last night, I still felt cautious and was being less physical with her. Or maybe she was being less physical with me and I was reacting cautiously. Either way, our pose looked anything but natural. Finally she leaned back against me and said in a tone that could have been flippant or earnest—I couldn't discern which—"It's okay if you act like you like me."

Without saying anything I put my arm around her. Rachel made the man take about a dozen pictures. She thanked him, then sat back down on the rock next to me and offered me a bottle of water. "Have some water."

"I'm okay."

"Drink," she said. "That's an order."

I took the bottle and drank half of it, then handed it back. "Happy?"

"Why wouldn't I be happy?" she said, standing. "I'm with you." She took my hand. "Let's go."

It was almost one when we got back to the hotel. I took a quick shower, then went out to the suite's living room. Rachel was waiting for me. We walked out to the front. I had called for my car and it was parked next to the valet desk.

"Do you need me to look up the address again?" Rachel asked.

"No. I've got it."

I pulled out of the resort's parking lot, and we headed off for Mesa.

It was Sunday and the Phoenix traffic was considerably lighter than it had been the day before. We arrived at my father's house ten minutes early. This time a white Subaru Impreza was parked in the driveway.

"Nervous?" Rachel asked.

I looked at her and forced a smile. "Why would I be nervous?"

She looked at me sympathetically. "What are you most nervous about?"

"I don't know. I mean, why am I even here?"

"The same reason I'm looking for my mother. You want to know yourself."

"I'm not him."

"No, but he's part of you."

I took a deep breath. "All right. Let's get this over with." I looked at her. "You're okay waiting in the car? I may be a while."

"That's all right. If you're long, I'll go for a walk."

"I'll leave the keys."

She grinned. "You mean, just in case we need to make a quick getaway."

I grinned back. "Exactly."

I opened my door. I walked up to the front of the house. The front door opened before I could ring the bell. My father stood in the doorway. I knew it was him instantly. He was still handsome, though he was completely bald. Actually, he had no facial hair, including eyebrows and eyelashes. My mind was flooded with a myriad of thoughts. *Cancer. Was he dying? Was this why he was so eager to see me? Deathbed repentance?*

Other than his lack of hair he looked healthy. He had bright eyes and a slight paunch of a stomach that comfortably filled out his khaki slacks and the short-sleeved Tommy Bahamas Hawaiian shirt he was wearing. For a moment neither of us spoke. Then his eyes welled. "Jacob."

I swallowed, my feelings spinning around like a wheel of fortune, waiting to land on something. "Scott."

We just stood there, neither of us sure what to do next. His wife, or at least the woman I'd spoken with the day before, walked up behind him. She was smiling. "Scott, why don't you ask your son in?"

It was like he had suddenly woken from a trance. "Of course. Come in. Please."

"Thank you." I stepped inside. The house was cool and bright inside. Skylights allowed the sun in and the interior design was modern and clean.

"Can I get you something to drink?" Scott said.

"Sure. I'll have a beer if you have one."

"I'll get it," the woman said.

"This is my wife, Gretchen," Scott said.

"We met yesterday," I said.

"It's good to see you again," she said. She turned to Scott. "Did you want something to drink?"

"Please," he said. "A beer too." He turned back to me. "So, have a seat." He gestured to a couch, a light-gray sectional with chrome legs and bright-crimson accent pillows. On one of the side tables was an eight-by-ten framed photograph of my father and me. We were standing on the porch of my childhood home, me in a coat and hat, my father holding my hand.

Lying on the glass coffee table in front of us, next to a porcelain figurine of Santa Claus, was a hardcover copy of my latest book. I guessed he had put it there so I would see it. Probably the photograph as well.

I sat down, and he sat close to me in a matching chaise. His eyes were still red. I could tell that he felt awkward, but I could also tell that he was glad to see me.

Still, neither of us knew what to say. It's not like there's some approved script for this. I thought, *It's a shame I haven't written about something like this in one of my books. At least I'd have something to fall back on*.

Scott was the first to bridge the gap. "So, what brings you to Phoenix?"

"You," I said.

He just nodded.

"How have you been?" I asked.

"I'm okay." He gestured to his head. "Lost all my hair."

"Cancer?"

"Yeah. Testicular. That chemo took all my hair."

"Did it help?"

"The doctors think they got it all. Old age aside, I feel pretty good."

"That's good," I said.

His head bobbed a little in agreement. "So, you live in Coeur d'Alene?"

"How did you know?"

He gestured to my book. "It's in the back of your book." He smiled. "I've read your books. All of them. They're excellent. You certainly didn't get that talent from me."

Gretchen walked in with two mugs filled with a dark amber beer. "This is Scott's favorite."

"Thank you," I said.

"Thank you, honey," Scott said.

After she left, I took a drink and said, "You always keep my book on the table?"

He grinned. "I put it out because you were coming."

"Honesty," I said, nodding. "And the picture of me?"

"No, that's always been there. Has since we moved here twenty years ago."

I let that sink in. "So, what are you doing now for work?"

"I'm semiretired, but I still do a little in social work. I'm a consultant. I work with hospitals and their mental health workers. I was in Tucson yesterday. It keeps me busy. And you? Book writing keep you busy?"

"Book writing, promoting, all the junk that comes with it."

"It sounds exciting."

"It has its moments."

The moment fell into silence. We both took another drink. Then Scott leaned back in his chair. "Thank you for coming. When Gretchen told me that you had come by, well, I didn't get much sleep last night. I was hoping to see you at your mother's funeral. I wasn't surprised that I didn't, but I was hoping. I hear she left you the house."

"I've been cleaning it."

He looked at me curiously. "Why?"

"Because it's a mess. She was a hoarder."

"I know; I meant, why you? You're an important man. You could hire someone to do that."

"I guess I thought I'd dig through the relics myself. Maybe answer some questions."

"I can see it being cathartic," he said. "Has it helped?"

I took a drink, then set the mug down on the napkin. "Not really. But maybe it's good to confront the pain."

He nodded knowingly. "Would you like to ask me anything?"

I looked at him for a moment. Then the words just shot out of my mouth, the verbal equivalent of projectile vomiting. "Yeah. Why did you leave me there?"

The words hung like smoke in the air between us. He looked down and his face fell with sorrow. He took a drink, wiped his mouth, then took another. Then he looked at me with red eyes. "Because I was stupid. At the time, I thought it was for the best." He exhaled. "The road to hell is paved with good intentions, right?"

He shook his head. "The thing is, I was a mess myself. Ruth blamed me for Charles's death. I blamed myself as well. I felt like I had already taken one son from her. I couldn't take another child from her. Not that the state would have let me anyway. Men don't often end up with the children, I knew that."

He breathed out slowly. "When I first told her that I wanted a divorce and I wanted to take you with me, she said to me, 'You want to take another child from me? You want to kill him too?'"

I swallowed.

"I couldn't do it. I had no right to do it. I had visitation rights, but I didn't take them. Not that I didn't want them—I desperately missed you—but because I had lost the ability to see you. I was so filled with grief and guilt that I did the worst thing I could do. I started drinking." He looked at me. "Long story short, four years later, I cleaned up. I remarried and went back into the field.

"I desperately wanted to see you, but it had been so long by then that I couldn't see how to do it without causing you pain." He looked me in the eyes. "In my profession I'd counseled clients who suddenly had a parent come back into their lives, and sometimes it just really messed with them. It caused them more pain, not less. It just didn't seem fair to put you through that. I didn't feel I had the right to."

His expression grew still more serious. "You have to understand that I honestly didn't know about Ruth's condition. I had no idea what she was doing to you. Years later, when I found out that she might be abusive, I contacted a lawyer about getting custody of you. I even called my old friends at DCFS to see if I could pull some strings. Then I called her. I told her that I was going to take you. That was a mistake. She freaked out. The next time I called, you were gone. You had run away."

"I didn't run away," I said. "She kicked me out. I came home one day and everything I owned was in the yard."

"I'm so sorry," he said, shaking his head. "Even when I tried to help, I failed you." Suddenly his eyes filled with tears. "I'm so sorry I wasn't stronger. I know, at this point, that saying I'm sorry is absurd. Way too little, way too late." He looked again into my eyes as a tear fell down his cheek. "I don't expect you to forgive me. I don't expect anything from you. But for what it's worth, I really am sorry."

His apology washed over me without effect. The moment fell into deep silence.

After a few moments he said, "I tried to find you, you know. I never forgot about you. I just thought I was doing the right thing. From where I was coming from, it made sense. Ruth had always been a good mother. She was a better mother than I was a father. She was a good person. At least when I knew her.

"And she loved you both. Losing Charles was the most difficult thing she had ever gone through. I could understand her turning on me—I guess she needed someone to blame—but I never imagined that she would turn on you."

He breathed out heavily. "In hindsight, I wish I had stayed with her. For both of your sakes. But hindsight's always twenty-twenty, isn't it?"

In spite of my pain, I slowly nodded. Then I looked into his eyes. "I hated you."

"I would expect that," he said softly. "You have every reason to hate me. I failed you. And I can't give you back what you lost." He grimaced and wiped his eyes. Then he looked back up at me. "If there's anything I can do for you now, I'll do it." His eyes welled up again. "Even if you tell me to stay out of your life."

The moment again fell into silence. My father had poured out everything he had, and now it was my turn to respond. My mind reeled. I wasn't sure what I had expected in coming back to see him, but it wasn't this. I realized that there was some part of me that had hoped he would attempt to justify his actions, giving me justification for my hatred and anger. But he hadn't. He was humble and self-deprecating. He had thrown himself under the proverbial bus.

As I sat there, Elyse's words about truth came back to me. In less than an hour, my perspective on the world, past, present, and future, had changed. In all honesty, had I been in his position, I might have done the exact same thing he had. I could fault his failure—even his wisdom—but not his heart. He had clearly suffered deeply for his mistakes. He was still suffering. I felt no reason to add to his pain. Again Elyse's words came to me: *Grace. Grace.*

As I looked at him, he seemed different to me. It was like looking in a mirror. We were the same person, in the same place, seeking the same thing—peace and reconciliation with the past. There was no point in dragging this into the future.

"There is something you can do," I finally said.

"Anything," he replied.

"There's someone I want you to meet. She's outside in the car."

CHAPTER
Twenty-Two

September 24, 1986

Dear Diary,

My baby was hiccuping today. It's so strange to think that she has a life of her own. I wish I could be in there with her, where no one could see me. Today Jacob asked me if I had ever been to the moon. I said, "No." He said, "I have." I said, "What was it like?" He said, "Charles was there."

I love that little boy.

Noel

Scott looked at Rachel curiously as I led her into the house.

"This is Rachel," I said.

He offered his hand. "It's nice to meet you."

"Thank you. Likewise."

"Please sit."

Rachel and I sat down on the couch. Scott sat back in the chaise. "So, are you two . . . married?"

"No," I said. "Rachel's a friend."

"Sorry. You make a good couple."

Rachel smiled. "You're not the first to think that."

"Can I get you a drink?"

"I'm okay," she said.

"Jacob said you had something to ask me."

"Yes." She glanced at me, then back at my father. "Did you have a young woman living with you about the time you lost Charles?"

My father just stared at her for a moment, then said, "That's why you look so familiar. You look exactly like your mother."

Rachel took a sharp breath. I reached over and squeezed her hand.

"The answer to your question is yes. She was a young lady named Noel Ellis. She was from Logan, Utah. She was almost three months pregnant when she came to live with us."

I glanced over at Rachel. She was nearly shaking. "Do you know where she lives now?"

"It's been a little while. After she got married, she moved to Provo. We lost touch after that, but up to that point she would call fairly regularly."

"Why?" I asked.

My father looked at me. "Because of you, I think. She loved you. Of course I was still around at the time, but she had seen how hard your mother was taking things. I think she had better intuition than I did."

"If she got married, her last name changed," Rachel said.

"Right," Scott said. "She married a guy named King. I think his first name was Keith. Maybe Kevin." He leaned back in his chair and finished his drink. Then he said,

"Noel King. Unless she got divorced and moved out of state, it shouldn't be hard to find her."

"Thank you so much," Rachel said.

"I'm glad to help."

Just then Gretchen walked in. "Hi, I'm feeling left out." She walked up to me. "Welcome home, Jacob."

"Thank you," I said.

She turned to Rachel. "And what is your name, dear?"

"Rachel," she said. "It's nice to meet you."

"And?" she said, wagging her finger between us. "You two are . . ."

"Just friends," Rachel said, a little too quickly.

My heart panged a little.

"Oh," Gretchen replied. "Pity. You look so cute together."

"That's what I said," Scott said. "I just didn't use the word *cute*."

Gretchen smiled. "Well, food is almost ready. I'm broiling salmon and I'm told that I'm quite good at it, so if you would like to eat with us, we would be delighted."

I looked at Rachel.

"I love salmon," she said.

"Love to," I said.

"Wonderful. Rachel, would you like to come into the kitchen while I finish? I could use some girl talk."

"Of course," she said, standing.

After they left, I looked at my father. "Gretchen seems nice."

"She's a really fine woman." Then he looked down. "I'm

a lucky man, Jacob. I've married two fine women in my life. I'm grateful for both of them."

I looked at him quizzically. "Even after all Mom did?"

"What she did?" he repeated gently. "She gave me love. She gave me you." His eyes welled. "You should know, I wept at her funeral. But she died long before that. I knew the woman she was, Jacob. And I still love that woman. I always will." He shook his head. "She had my sympathy, even my pity for what she became, but not my disdain. She deserves that respect." Then he looked at me again. "She gave me you and Charles. What more could I ask for?"

CHAPTER

Twenty-Three

October 22, 1986

Dear Diary,

I'm more tired these days. Carrying around this bowling ball doesn't help, but it's more than that. I just want to lie in bed sometimes, like Mrs. Churcher, but I can't. I'm doing all the cooking and cleaning now. I feel like I'm Jacob's only mother. Sometimes Scott helps if he's not late. He's very busy at work, though I wonder if maybe it's hard being home with his wife the way she is, so he stays away. He's so sad too. I know he blames himself for what happened. Why does life have to be so hard? I hope my skin stops itching. It drives me crazy.

Noel

I was glad that I had said yes to the dinner invitation, not just because the food was remarkable but because Gretchen had undoubtedly spent the better part of the day in the kitchen preparing for us with little more than a slim hope that we might dine with them.

We started off our meal with a light arugula and avocado salad, followed by salmon with glazed sweet carrots, garlic green beans, and crispy roasted new potatoes. For dessert we had something Gretchen called a strawberry cool brûlée, which was something like a crème brûlée but without the cooking or caramelized sugar on top.

After we ate, we sat around the table and talked. Scott brought out wine, a four-year-old bottle of Rioja Blanco he had been saving for a special occasion. It paired perfectly with the dinner. Even Rachel had a little. She didn't have much, just a glass, but it seemed to immediately affect her.

Rachel said to Gretchen, "I don't really drink. Actually, I never drink."

"You shouldn't have much, then," Gretchen said.

"I'll just have a little more," she replied.

My father filled her cup half-full. "There you go, dear."

"Thank you." She turned to me. "I'm such a lush."

We all laughed.

It was a pleasant evening, and, frankly, not at all how I'd expected it to go. As the evening waned, my father said, "You need to tell me something. Even though, technically, you did live in the same house, you never met. So how did the two of you hook up?"

Rachel looked at me and smiled widely. "It was my fault. I kept coming to the house to see if I could find someone to tell me about my mother. One day I came by and there was Jacob. It was . . . fortuitous."

"It was fortuitous," I said. "That was a good day."

Rachel smiled. "For both of us."

I cleared my throat. "Rachel's engaged."

Gretchen turned to her. "Oh? Who's the lucky man?"

"His name is Brandon," Rachel said. "He's from St. George. He's an accountant."

"Well, Brandon must be an amazing guy," my father said. "Not just because Jacob is tough competition, but because you are definitely a catch."

"You're embarrassing me," Rachel said, smiling. Then she said to me, "Do you think I'm a catch?"

"Of course I do."

She looked at me with a peculiar expression. Scott and Gretchen must have noticed it as well, because no one spoke for a moment. Then Gretchen said, "Would anyone like some coffee? I have decaf."

"No, thank you," Rachel said.

"Thank you," I said. "But it's been a long day. We should probably get back to the hotel."

"It's been more than a long day. It's been a really good day."

"Hear, hear," I said, lifting my glass.

At the front door Scott said to me, "Thank you. For giving me a chance."

I nodded slowly. "Thank you for the truth. And what you gave Rachel."

"It was my pleasure."

"I'm curious. What you told us about Rachel's mother—are you supposed to share that information?"

He shook his head. "No. That was not kosher."

"Can you get in trouble with the state?"

He shrugged. "I suppose."

"But still you shared it."

"I had just told you that if there was *anything* I could do for you, I would do it. That was no time to renege on an offer. So, you asked who she was, I told you."

"Thank you. You have no idea how much this means to her."

"You have no idea how much this means to *me*. I'm just glad I was around for it."

"Me too," I said.

He suddenly sighed. In a softer voice he said, "Tell Rachel not to get her hopes too high."

"Why is that?"

"Noel's parents went to such great lengths to hide her pregnancy that they probably wanted it kept secret. It's possible that when she married, she never told her husband that she'd had a child. It wouldn't be the first time I'd run across that in marriage counseling."

I nodded thoughtfully. "I'll tell her. Thank you."

"When can I see you again?" he asked.

"You name the time."

"You're the busy one. You say when, and we'll be there. Gretchen and I like to drive. I've never been big on flying."

I nodded. "So that's where I got it."

CHAPTER

Twenty-Four

October 29, 1986

Dear Diary,

Two days ago I thought I was going into labor. Mr. Churcher had to come home from work and drive me and Jacob to the hospital. They said it was false labor, something called Braxton Hicks. (Of course it was named after a man. Like he ever had it.) I wouldn't want a false labor named after me. I was sorry to inconvenience Mr. Churcher. Little Jacob was so confused. He didn't like it when they took me back into the checkup room and wouldn't let him go with me. He started crying. He didn't even want to be with his father. He wanted me.

Noel

Rachel was the happiest I'd seen her since we'd met. The night air was cool, so I opened the car's front windows a few inches to bring in fresh air. As we drove back to our hotel, I said, "What a night. I thought it was going to be awful. Instead, it was perfect."

"He was so happy to see you," she said. Then she added,

"I'm happy to see you." I glanced over at her and she suddenly laughed. "I feel so good."

"It's the wine," I said.

"I might have to do this more."

"Yeah. Well, not tonight."

"How come?"

"Because you've had enough."

As we neared the resort Rachel became less talkative and I wondered if the alcohol was making her sleepy. I handed my keys to the valet, then took Rachel by the arm and walked into the hotel.

As we walked down the long corridor to our suite, she laid her head on my shoulder. I put my arm around her. We walked inside our room, then Rachel turned to me, a soft smile warming her face. "Thank you for helping me find my mother."

"You're welcome," I said. "We helped each other."

She looked into my eyes. "Did you mean what you said?"

"What did I say?"

"Do you really think I'm a catch?"

"Yes. You are. Not just because you're insanely beautiful but because you're a really good person. You're very sweet."

She giggled. "I am sweet," she said, touching my chest with her finger. "Do you like me?"

"Of course."

"I don't think Brandon likes me. I think he wants to marry me, but I think he would change a lot of things about me if he could. I think he's going to put a leash on me."

I chuckled. "He'd be a fool to do so. And you have definitely had too much to drink."

"I only had a little."

"I know. But for you a little is a lot."

Her eyes softened with a childlike vulnerability. "Do you love me?"

The question had more power than she could have known. My heart throbbed in my chest. I looked into her eyes. "Yes."

"I love you too. I love you more than anyone I've ever known." Then she leaned into me and we kissed. Softly at first, then with growing passion and power. After a couple of minutes she stepped back from me and grabbed my hand. "Come here." She led me into her bedroom and we both fell over on the bed. We drew together like magnets, her soft, full lips dissolving into mine. Then she reached over and began to undress me. I took her hands and stopped her.

"No," I said, sitting up. "We can't do this."

"Of course we can," she said breathlessly. "I want to do this."

"No. You'll hate me tomorrow. You're engaged to another man."

"I don't want to be engaged anymore."

"You're in no condition to decide that right now. I'm not going to lose you by taking advantage of you."

She started to cry. "You won't lose me."

"Yes, I will. Your guilt will eat you alive. You won't want it to, but it will."

Her wet eyes pleaded with me. "But don't you want me?"

"More than I've ever wanted anyone." I kissed her again. Then, with our eyes still locked on each other, I stood. "We'll talk in the morning, Rachel. We'll make plans in the morning."

I didn't just walk out of her room, I walked out of the suite. I took a brief walk around the property to cool myself off. I was pretty sure that I wanted her more than she wanted me. But I was also sure that I wanted her for more than just one night. And after her last meltdown, it was clear to me that her guilt was bigger than she could handle.

Later that night, as I lay in bed, the quote from Hamlet came to mind: "Thus conscience does make cowards of us all."

CHAPTER

Twenty-Five

November 25, 1986

Dear Diary,

I've missed a few weeks of writing. I just didn't feel like writing anything. I had nothing new. Thanksgiving is this Thursday. No one has said a word about it. I know Mrs. Churcher won't do anything. Even though I'm tired, I told Mr. Churcher that I would be happy to make the Thanksgiving meal. He said that would be nice. I'll take Jacob shopping with me tomorrow. I don't know how to make pumpkin pie, but I think it will be easy. One pie will be enough for us. My mother is very good at baking pies. She'll make apple, mincemeat, pumpkin, and cherry. There will be a big turkey. The whole family and Aunt Genielle and her two hundred children will be there. I miss my family. I wonder if they'll talk about me at dinner and ask how I'm doing at school. My mom will say, Oh, you know Noel, she always gets good grades.

I don't think anyone around here is very grateful for anything these days. If a meteor came down and landed on this house, everyone would probably be better off. Except Jacob. If a meteor came down, I would put my body over his and try to shield him. I would give my life for this little boy. What am I thankful for this Thanksgiving? I'm thankful for him.

Noel

DECEMBER 19

I woke the next morning with a light hangover. I had slept in a little. It was almost nine. Hangover or not, a big smile crossed my face. I felt like I'd just won the lottery. Rachel wanted me too.

I pulled on some shorts and a T-shirt, then walked to her room. At first I slowly opened the door, trying not to let in too much light. To my surprise, the room was filled with light. The blinds were open and the room was empty.

"Rachel?"

She probably just went out for a walk, I thought. I walked into her bedroom. "Rachel." I checked her bathroom. Her suitcase was gone. Everything was gone. She was gone.

I walked back out to the front of the suite. On the counter next to the door was a note.

Dear Jacob,

I woke in the middle of the night feeling dark and heartsick. Most of all, ashamed. What am I doing here, sharing a room with another man? What kind of woman sneaks off on a trip with another man, then tries to seduce him? I am so, so ashamed. I tried to tell myself that last night was an accident, that it was the wine, but I know the truth. I didn't need to see your father. There's nothing he could tell me that you couldn't have relayed to me. The truth is, I wanted to go with you because I wanted to be with you. And that's wrong. It's wrong that I like that you get jealous of Brandon. It's wrong that I'd rather be with you than him. Most of all, it's wrong that after all of Brandon's trust in me, I chose to cheat on him.

Last night you told me that you loved me because I was a really good person. Obviously, I'm not. I want to be. But I'm not. You deserve a good woman. You did the right thing last night. I didn't. I'm not the woman I thought I was. Thank you for respecting me enough to not make my sin worse. Please forgive me. I will never stop thinking of you. With love always,

Rachel

P.S. Thank you for letting me read my mother's journal. I wanted to take it with me, but it's not mine. I realize that she belongs to you too.

I put the note back down on the counter, then kicked the cupboard door beneath it.

CHAPTER

Twenty-Six

November 27, 1986

Dear Diary,

Thanksgiving was actually nice. Even Mrs. Churcher came out for a little while. She had some turkey and stuffing and mashed potatoes. She thanked me, then went back into her bedroom. Mr. Churcher was in pain. I could see it. After dinner I went to do the dishes, and he came in to help me. He was standing next to me, and I could see that he was crying. I put my arms around him, and he laid his head on my shoulder and cried hard. I suppose it would have looked very weird, but grief isn't a beauty pageant. Jacob grabbed onto my leg. (I think he may have been jealous.) I've wondered where God has been in all this, but maybe I was supposed to come to this home at this time, because some days I feel like I'm the only thing holding it together. As I put Jacob to bed, he asked me why we had a Thanksgiving. I told him about the Pilgrims, then said, We do it so we can remember what we have to be thankful for. He asked me what thankful was. I said, Thankful is what we are glad we have. And he said, I'm thankful for you. I almost started crying. But then he said, And whipped cream. I kissed him and laughed.

On the pregnancy front, my baby dropped. And my boobs are getting big and heavy. I feel like someone has commandeered my body. Oh, wait, someone did.

Noel

It was time to go home. Not just back to Salt Lake, but really home. Back to Coeur d'Alene.

The traffic out of town was miserable. Actually the whole drive back to Salt Lake was miserable. Almost as bad as flying. In fact, worse, since I could sedate myself on a plane trip and driving lasted ten times longer. I was tempted to abandon my car in Phoenix and catch the next flight out to Salt Lake.

Driving the same route back that we'd come down on was like watching a rerun of a canceled show. I could practically hear Rachel's voice the whole way. *This is where Rachel said this. This is where Rachel laughed about that.* It was miserable. And the most despairing part was that life wasn't going to stop being miserable anytime soon. Because the woman I had fallen in love with was going to marry a manipulative little man out of guilt or duty or religious obligation and be miserable for the rest of her life. And I was going to think about her for the rest of my life and hurt for her.

My heart hadn't hurt this badly for many years.

Laurie called as I was passing through Panguitch, a small town in southern Utah.

"Where are you?"

"I'm driving home," I said.

"Home to Coeur d'Alene?"

"No. Salt Lake."

"You don't sound well."

"What do I sound like?"

"You sound angry. Like you're about to go on a shooting spree."

"I'm thinking about it."

"So things didn't go well with your father."

"No, things went better than expected. But I lost Rachel."

"Who's Rachel?"

I hesitated. "She's no one."

Laurie knew better than to ask. "I'm really sorry. Is there anything I can do?"

"No. I just need space."

"You got it. Just drive safe. Be safe. And let me know when you're back in Coeur d'Alene. Otherwise you can call anytime. I'm here for you."

"Thank you."

"Bye. Kisses. Take care of yourself."

"Bye."

I drove fast. In fact, I made it back to the Grand America Hotel before nine p.m. It was cold and bleak in Salt Lake, which pretty much matched my temperament. I didn't know what to do. Actually, I did. I needed to go back home, get good and drunk for a week, then get on with my life, hoping that the embers of my feelings for Rachel would soon grow cold.

In spite of my decision, I still had things to do in Salt Lake. I needed to sign papers with Brad so we could list the house. And then I was going to see my dream lady. I planned to do both as soon as possible, then retreat to my previous, lonely life.

As I got in bed I thought, *At least there's probably a book in this.*

CHAPTER

Twenty-Seven

December 3, 1986

Dear Diary,

This morning I helped Jacob write his Christmas list to Santa. He asked me what I was getting. I said, A baby. He said, That's like Jesus. He was a Christmas present too. I don't know how he came up with that. No one here talks about Jesus. Then he said, Jesus got golden franks for Christmas. What is your baby getting? It came out without thinking. I said, A new mother. Jacob asked me why I was crying.

Noel

DECEMBER 20

I woke at nine fifteen, just missing a phone call. I rolled over and checked my phone. It was Brad Campbell. I called him back.

"Churcher," he said. "How are you?"

"Good."

"I dropped by the house on Sunday but you weren't there."

"I was in Phoenix."

"Lucky you. I could use a respite from this weather. Maybe I'll find an excuse to fly to Phoenix. Or St. George."

His mention of St. George brought Rachel to mind. And pain. "Do you have some papers for me?"

"Yes I do. I can bring them by your hotel if you like."

"That would be great."

"Do you have time for lunch? The Grand has a nice restaurant."

"Sure," I said. "A late lunch."

"How late?"

I thought about it. "Two. I'm checking out today."

"Two o'clock is good for me. Headed home, huh?"

"I've got just one more thing to do before I leave."

"Well, it's been nice having you here. I hope it was a memorable visit."

"It was definitely that," I said. "I'll see you at two."

I skipped working out and breakfast, opting instead for a protein bar, then took a shower. I sat on the floor of the shower and let the water cascade around me. *What had I done wrong?* I had tried to do the right thing. The hard thing. And it had blown up on me. Then again, maybe there was no way for things to work out. Had I not done the right thing, I couldn't imagine how great her guilt would be.

I kept checking my phone, hoping that she had called, but she hadn't. She wasn't going to call.

I left my bags at the bell stand and met Brad at the hotel's Garden Café. Shortly after our food arrived, Brad asked, "So what are your plans with the house?"

"I'm just going to sell it," I said.

"Do you need a real estate agent? A local one?"

"That would help. Do you know a good one?"

"I know a few. They'll take good care of you." He lifted his leather portfolio. "I brought the documents." He laid a stack of papers on the table next to my food. Each of the papers had various Post-it arrow flags directing me where to sign.

"I don't have a pen," I said.

"You can have mine." He handed me a black resin pen inscribed with the name of his firm.

I signed all the documents, then handed the papers back to him.

"Thank you, sir. And that concludes our official business together. If you ever need a lawyer, you know where to find me."

"It's already in my phone," I said, then lifted his pen. "And it's right here."

"Just don't lose that pen," he said.

I reached for the check, and he put his hand on it. "I've got it. Business expense."

"Thank you for lunch. Actually, thank you for everything. Especially for taking care of my mother during her last days."

He looked at me with a peculiarly satisfied smile. "You did get a lot done, didn't you?"

We said good-bye and I drove my car up to the front doors and had the bell captain bring out my luggage. I opened the tailgate and he put my suitcase in the back. I unzipped the suitcase and took out the leather diary. Then I slammed the tailgate shut and handed the bell captain a ten-dollar tip. He thanked me. "Come back soon," he said.

"Not likely," I replied. "Have a good day."

I climbed into my car, turned the radio on to Christmas music, then rolled out of the hotel's circular drive and headed south to find Noel.

With a name like Noel King, she wasn't hard to track down. There were only two Noel Kings in the United States, and only one in Utah.

She no longer lived in Provo. Since her marriage, she had moved nine miles south to a small town called Spanish Fork. It was fifty-two miles south on I-15 from downtown Salt Lake, less than an hour away. Ironically, Rachel and I had driven past the town on our way to Phoenix.

Spanish Fork is a small town of about thirty-five thousand people. It wasn't difficult finding the King home. Besides living in my dreams for the last thirty-plus years, Noel King lived on a real street wonderfully called Wolf Hollow Drive, just south of the town's Centennial Park, which was sandwiched between the town's only cemetery and their only junior high.

The house was even smaller than my mother's, a box-shaped tiled home with a steeply pitched roof and a long front porch.

There was as much snow on the ground here as there was in Salt Lake, but the driveway was shoveled clean and dry, as was the walkway and sidewalk in front of the house.

The house was decorated for Christmas with multicolored lights strung across the length of the house and, in the front yard, an almost life-sized nine-piece model of the nativity in faded plastic. There was Joseph and Mary kneeling next to a manger with baby Jesus. There were three Wise Men, a shepherd, and a camel and donkey. It was an ambitious display for such a small yard.

I was parked across the street and still admiring the crèche when a utility van pulled into the home's driveway. The van was wrapped with a cartoon picture of a man wearing a crown and holding an orange pipe wrench like a scepter. To the side of the cartoon were the words

KEVIN KING PLUMBING

THE PLUMBER KING FOR YOUR CASTLE'S ROOTER AND PLUMBING NEEDS

A heavyset man in Levi's and a striped denim shirt got out of the van and walked in the side door of the home.

"My angel's married to the king of plumbing," I said.

I grabbed the diary, got out of the car, and walked up the concrete path to the front door, which was adorned with a large pine-needle wreath with red ribbon and gold and blue baubles. There was a piece of electrical tape over the doorbell, so I knocked. A few minutes later the man I'd just seen enter the home opened the door. He was plump and red-faced with a five-o'clock shadow. There was a label sewn on his shirt that read KEVIN.

The first thing he said was, "That your Porsche parked across the street?"

I glanced furtively back at my car. "Yes."

"One of them Porsche SUVs. I tell ya, they'll make an SUV outta just about anything these days. Wouldn't surprise me a bit to see a Rolls SUV. So what that set you back, fifty, sixty grand?"

"It's the Turbo S, so it was about one sixty."

I thought his jaw would drop off. "Holy Mother of . . . You must be made of money, sir. I'm clearly in the wrong business. What is it that you do?"

"I write books. Novels."

"I'm gonna have to try my hand at writing books one of these days. I got stories, I tell ya. The things I seen in houses. Turn your skin blue. So what brings you by today?"

"I'm looking for Noel King. I'm guessing she's your wife."

"What you want with my wife? Never mind, you can have her. I'll trade you straight up for the Porsche." He laughed at himself. "No? I didn't think so. I'll call her." He turned around. "No-el. Someone's at the door for ya." He turned back to me. "We don't get many strangers coming around here, just your usual alarm or water purifier salesmen, but last few days we're two for two. Got you today and a young woman last night."

Rachel.

"A young woman came by yesterday?"

"Pretty gal. Just a little mixed up. I figured she was probably smokin' some of that Colorado."

"Why is that?"

"Well, to begin with, she asked my wife if she had a child thirty years ago. I told her that she wasn't even married back then. Noel felt bad for the young lady. She told her that she was sorry, but she must be mistaken."

I recalled the warning my father had given me as I left his house. "What did the young woman do?"

"She got all teary-eyed and just looked at my wife for the longest time. It was kind of uncomfortable. Then she walked away. Funny thing, she actually did look a lot like my wife. At least the way she looked in her younger years. Almost could have been twins. Sure shook up the missus, though. She cried all night."

"You're sure she wasn't her daughter?"

The man looked at me as if I were dumb as a brick. He crossed his arms at his chest. "Course I'm sure. I've been married to her for twenty-seven years. I think I would've known if I got her pregnant. Heck, Noel can't even have children."

"You don't have children?"

"I just said that. She can't have children. She's barren."

"She's barren," I said.

He grinned. "Well, I assure you, the plumbing's all workin' in this house. And I know plumbing."

I hid my growing annoyance. "You are the king of plumbing."

He laughed.

I heard approaching footsteps as a woman walked up behind the man. My chest froze. It was her. My dream woman in flesh and blood. She looked younger than I had expected. In fact, she was still recognizable from the photograph I'd found in the diary. She still looked pretty.

For years I had wondered what this moment, if it ever came, would be like. I had thought it might be like meeting a favorite actor or rock star. But it wasn't like that at all. Sure, it was surreal in its own way. But it wasn't uncomfortable. I guess it was because she didn't seem like a stranger to me. How could she? She had been with me for all these years.

She looked at me with a peculiar expression, and I wondered if some part of her recognized me as well. Unfortunately, her husband didn't leave but stood there like a curious child not wanting to be left out.

"May I help you?" she asked kindly.

"You're Noel Ellis?"

"Ellis was my maiden name," she said with a guarded smile. "And you are?"

I reached out my hand, my eyes locked on hers. "My name is Jacob Christian Churcher."

She responded as if electricity had shot through me and shocked her. She dropped my hand. She looked afraid.

"I'm sorry," she stammered. "Do I know you?"

I glanced over at the plumber, then back at her. I pitied her that even now she felt that she had to live her life as a lie. "Actually, you probably don't remember me," I lied for her sake. "But you were briefly friends with my parents. I just wanted to tell you that my mother, Ruth Churcher, passed away."

She swallowed. "I'm sorry to hear that," she said. "And your father?"

"He's still alive," I said. "He's doing well."

"Well, give him my condolences, please."

"Of course." For a moment I just looked at her. I was certain that she knew who I was. And I was pretty sure that she knew that I knew that she knew who I was. So there we were, playing out a charade like actors on a front-porch stage with a one-plumber audience fueling the sham. I suddenly detested the man.

"All right," I finally said. "That's all I wanted to say. By the way, you should know something about that baby girl who was born in my parents' house. They named her Rachel. She's a good woman with a good heart. Just like her mother. Her mother would be proud of her." I looked into her eyes. "I just thought you might want to know that."

Her eyes welled up. The plumber looked at me like I was speaking Chinese, but Noel was clearly fighting her emotions, which still escaped in tears.

"Have a good day."

Noel wiped her eyes. "Good-bye," she said softly.

I was turning to go when suddenly something clicked inside me. Something angry and strong. Something unwilling to let the evil of the past win. I turned back around.

"Noel."

She looked intently into my eyes. "Yes?"

"There's something I need to tell you."

She looked at me expectantly.

"For almost as long as I can remember, I've dreamed of a lovely young woman who held me when my world was falling apart. She was the one woman who loved a scared little boy even when her own world was crashing down around her. That woman in my dreams held me in the dark when I was afraid. She kept me company when I was alone. And she loved me when I believed that I was unlovable."

My eyes suddenly welled up. "She was the best woman I have ever known. And I don't care if the world made her live a lie, but the truth of who she is is far too great to be put down by its shame and deceit. I love that woman with all my heart. And I told myself that if I ever saw her again, she would know that."

I lifted the diary. "This is yours, Noel. It belongs to you, not them. Not to the lie. You wrote in here that you would rather live an honest life than an admired one. You deserve both. It's your life, not theirs. It's your right to claim it." I offered her the book. "It's time to let go of the shame and walk free. The truth will set you free."

The moment was frozen. The plumber was utterly dumbstruck. But I saw something light in her eyes. Maybe it was courage. Maybe it was indignation. Maybe it was just exhaustion, but she reached down and took the diary. *Her* diary. Then she looked back up at me and said, "My dear, darling Jacob. My sweet Jacob." Tears fell down her face. "You have no idea how much I've worried about you." She moved forward and threw her arms around me. She cried for several minutes. Then, when she could speak, she said, "Please, Jacob. Rachel was here. Can you help me find my baby?"

CHAPTER

Twenty-Eight

December 10, 1986

Dear Diary,

Around me people are counting down the days until Christmas. I'm counting down the days until I give birth. Last night, Mr. Churcher, Jacob, and I watched A Christmas Carol on television. The one with George C. Scott. I feel like the young Ebenezer Scrooge, sent away to boarding school. My parents haven't reached out to me once. They're religious but not godly. Their religion is nothing more than an idol of their own making, an image. A façade. I used to be afraid that they wouldn't let me come back home. Now I have no desire to ever live under the same roof with them again.

Noel

Noel and I talked openly for the next hour. Kevin came and went, baffled by what was happening and totally clueless as to how to respond. I told her about how I had come down from Coeur d'Alene after my mother's death and found Rachel or, more correctly, how she had found me.

Noel said that she had driven by the old house a few

times. She even saw my mother once but didn't wave. She doubted that my mother would have even known who she was. As we talked she clutched the diary like an actor holding her Oscar. "I can't believe it came back," she said.

Finally I told her that I needed to go. "Rachel lives in southern Utah. In Ivins."

"I know Ivins," she said. "It's near St. George."

I nodded. "I can write her address down for you."

Noel turned to her husband. "Kevin, go get me a notepad from the kitchen."

"Sure." He stumbled off.

With Kevin gone, she looked a little more relaxed. "Thank you for not giving up on me. It is so good to see you. And Rachel." She shook her head. "I'd drive down to see her tonight but . . ." She paused and glanced back. "I think my husband and I have a lot to talk about."

"I'm sure you do. How will that go?"

"I don't know how it will go with him, but I know it's what I want." She looked into my eyes. "No, it's what I need. There comes a time when carrying the secret becomes more painful than the truth it's hiding. That's where I am. I just needed a reason to open up."

Kevin lumbered back out carrying a steno pad and a pen. "Here you go," he said, handing them to his wife.

"Thank you." She handed them to me. I checked my phone for Rachel's address and wrote it out on the pad. "I hope you can read that," I said, handing back the pad. "For a writer, my handwriting is horrific."

"It's fine," she said. She smiled. "The last time I saw you,

you were scribbling then too. You always had trouble coloring inside the lines."

"Some things never change," I said.

We hugged. Her embrace felt wonderful. Better than a dream. "Thank you," I said.

"No. Thank you. I love you."

I just looked at her and smiled. "I know. I really know. I love you too."

CHAPTER

Twenty-Nine

December 17, 1986

Dear Diary,

Today is my baby's due date. I can't believe she hasn't come yet. The doctor said that she was waiting for Christmas. I told him that being born on Christmas wasn't anything great. He laughed and said I should have thought about that last March. The shame returned. It always returns. I should have thought about a lot of things last March. I told him that I wasn't really thinking about Christmas back then. The truth was, I was only thinking about how much I wanted someone to love me.

Noel

The night I returned from Phoenix, I had looked up where Rachel said she lived. Ivins, Utah, is a bedroom community northwest of St. George, the fourth-largest city in Utah. The Ivins area was once populated by the Paiute Indians and was originally named Santa Clara Bench, but the residents later rejected that name and came up with *Ivins* after a Mormon apostle named Anthony Ivins, who said that he didn't object to their using his name as long as they spelled it right.

Ivins's climate, like St. George's, is typical of the desert southwest and significantly warmer than the rest of the state.

I took the St. George off-ramp at about a quarter to ten and drove west in the darkness toward Ivins, arriving just a few minutes past the hour. To me the landscape looked more like Sedona than Salt Lake. It took me just twenty minutes to find Rachel's home.

As she had told me, the home was older than those around it and, not surprisingly, more conservative in design and landscaping. It was one floor with a tan stucco exterior. The yard was all gravel rock and surrounded by a red cinder-block fence on both sides.

Even though it was only a little past ten, the house was dark, the only illumination being a single porch light and the ankle-high solar lights lining the walkway. I could see inside the house through a large picture window that had neither blinds nor curtains. Fortunately, Rachel's car was parked in the driveway.

I walked up to the house and knocked on the door. Twice. The second time I knocked, a hall light turned on. Then I heard footsteps shuffle up to the door. There was a short pause, followed by the sliding of a dead bolt. Then two more lights came on over the porch and the door opened to reveal an elderly man in a thick, umber terry-cloth robe. He was shorter than me, bald, with wire-rimmed glasses resting on the bridge of a sizable beak, and dark, bushy eyebrows that seemed as wild as an overgrown bush. All he needed was a pitchfork and he could stand in for the old man in *American Gothic*.

He pointedly glanced down at his watch, then said gruffly, "What do you need?"

"I'm here to see Rachel."

"Who are you?"

"I'm a friend of Rachel's."

He didn't flinch. "Rachel's already in bed."

"Sorry, I'm from Coeur d'Alene. It's an hour earlier there."

He didn't find my insight amusing.

"Sir, I just drove down from Salt Lake to see your daughter."

"Well, you're just going to have to drive back."

"I thought she was exaggerating," I muttered to myself.

"Excuse me?"

Just then I heard Rachel's voice. "Dad, who is it?"

He glanced over his shoulder, then back at me. I shrugged. "Sorry. Looks like I woke the baby."

Rachel walked up behind him. She froze when she saw me.

"He says he knows you," the old man said.

"He's a friend."

I looked at her.

"This is Jacob," she said softly.

"The guy?"

I looked at her. "The *guy*?"

"I need to talk to him," she said.

He looked at me with disdain, then said beneath his breath, "'As the dog returns to his vomit.'"

I looked him in the eyes. "Did you just call me a dog and your daughter vomit?"

Again, not amused. He turned and shuffled away.

I turned to Rachel. "The *guy*?"

"What are you doing here, Jacob?"

"The question is, what are you doing here?"

"I live here."

"You live here, or you're *incarcerated* here?"

She didn't answer.

"I saw your mother," I said.

Anger crossed her face. "So did I. She didn't know me."

"I know, she told me. She was sorry. It broke her heart."

"Yeah? Well, it broke my heart too. Do you know what it feels like to have your own mother reject you?"

"Yes. Actually, I do."

She paused. Then she said more softly, "At least my *warden* of a father isn't throwing me away like I was disposable."

"She was a scared teenager, Rachel. Tell me that life hasn't ever made you do something you didn't want to."

She took a deep breath, then exhaled slowly. "What do you want, Jacob?"

"You know what I want."

"And that is?"

"You left without saying good-bye."

"I said good-bye in the note."

"Now that's where I'm confused, because I write things all the time that people twist and manipulate, but when I tell someone that I love them more than anyone I've ever known and that I don't think my fiancé—"

"I'm engaged, Jacob."

"—I don't think my fiancé really likes me—"

"I was drunk."

"Sometimes it takes a little alcohol to be honest."

"I'm engaged."

"Engaged or not, I know the truth. So do you. You don't want to be with him. You want to be with me. And I want to be with you."

She started crying.

"Am I wrong?"

She just kept crying. When she could speak, she said, "What I want doesn't matter."

I looked at her in astonishment. "Then what does?"

"Doing what's *right*."

"And marrying someone you don't want to marry is right?"

She didn't answer.

"Come on, honey," I said gently. "I love you. I'll treat you the way you deserve to be treated."

Again she didn't answer. Finally, I said, "All right. Answer me this, and I'll leave you alone. If you hadn't already told him yes three years ago, would you still answer yes now?"

She just looked at me. After a long silence I said, "There's your answer."

"I didn't answer."

"If you have to think about whether you want to marry someone after being engaged for three years, you have your answer."

Her eyes again filled with tears. "I made a commitment."

"No, you made a commitment to make a commitment."

"It's the same thing!"

"No, it's not. If you were married, I wouldn't be standing here, and you know it. You know I would respect that."

She started crying harder.

"Rachel . . ."

Suddenly she shouted, "Yes!"

I looked at her. "What?"

"Yes. I would still say yes to him."

She looked as surprised by what she'd said as I was. I was breathless. She might as well have hit me in the stomach with a Louisville Slugger. After a moment I exhaled slowly. "Okay," I said softly. "Okay." The pain of her rejection jolted my entire body. It was like I was that child again, standing by the side of the road with my suitcase. I wanted to vomit.

Rachel looked at me, trembling. "Jacob . . ."

I couldn't look at her. I was unable to speak.

"Jacob."

I looked up at her slowly. "I'm sorry. I'll go."

I turned and slowly walked back to my car. Rachel was still standing in the doorway wiping her eyes as I backed out of the driveway.

In spite of the hour, I drove all the way back to Salt Lake City. When I got back to my mother's house, it was almost three in the morning.

[illegible]

[illegible] you [illegible]

here and you know it. You knew [illegible]

[illegible]

[illegible]

[illegible]

[illegible]

[illegible]

[illegible] slowly [illegible]

[illegible]

[illegible]

[illegible]

I looked [illegible]

[illegible] and slowly [illegible]

still [illegible]

end of the driveway.

[illegible]

almost [illegible]

CHAPTER Thirty

December 24, 1986

Dear Diary,

Today is my birthday. I turn eighteen today. No one here knows. Those who do know—my parents and Peter—don't care. I told little Jacob. Only Jacob. He smiled. It's Christmas Eve. I read tonight about Mary. The story is different to me this year, because I'm also with child. I'm also about to give birth among strangers. And they too will take my child from me. I'm not comparing myself with her—I'm too much a sinner. I'm comparing my pain. I hurt so much. And this home I'm in, my sweet Jacob—what will become of him? Mrs. Churcher is not well. She doesn't come out of her room anymore except at night. She's grown so thin. I don't know who will take care of Jacob now. I'm praying that his father will be what his son needs, because Ruth is gone. Maybe I shouldn't judge her. But I too am losing my baby—though my baby will still be out there, with someone else watching her grow up.

Noel

DECEMBER 21

I woke with the sun streaming in through my bedroom window, striping my face with light. I had gone to sleep in my bed. My childhood bed. It was appropriate. I hurt then too.

I realized that I had woken because someone was knocking at the door. I just lay there for a while. Then, when the pounding didn't stop, I got up, pulled on my pants and shirt, and walked barefoot out to the front room and opened the door.

Elyse stood on the porch, shivering a little in the cold. She held a small brown sack. I must have looked as bad as I felt because she studied me with obvious concern. "Are you okay?"

"Yeah. I just got up."

"I read you writers keep strange hours. It's past noon."

"It was a long night." I rubbed my eyes. "I got in around three."

"From Arizona?"

"No. Ivins." I looked at her. "Do you want to come in?"

"Please."

She walked inside, panning the room as she did. "It looks nice in here."

"Thanks." I motioned to the couch. "Have a seat."

"Thank you." She sat down on one end of the couch. I sat down in the middle.

"I was glad to see your car here this morning. I was afraid you'd gone home and I would never see you again."

"I'm leaving this afternoon. But I wouldn't have left without saying good-bye."

"That makes me glad." She looked around. "You really transformed this place. It hasn't looked like this for twenty-something years." She looked back at me. "Did you find your father?"

"Yes."

"How did that go?"

"It went well. It was like you said it would be."

"I'm glad for that too." She looked at me. "But you look sad."

"Not everything worked out."

"The girl?"

I raked my hand back through my hair. "Yes."

She nodded. "It's always the girl, isn't it? But then, that's what you write about."

"I would never write this story. But it doesn't matter. That's not why I came back."

She looked at me thoughtfully, then asked, "Why did you come back, Jacob?"

I took a deep breath. "I still don't know. I was looking for answers."

"Answers to what?"

I couldn't answer her. She looked at me for a moment, then said, "You'll never find the answer to what you're really looking for."

"You know what I'm *really* looking for?"

"I'm pretty sure that I do. It's the same thing your friend

Rachel came here looking for. You want to know why you weren't worthy of your mother's love."

I just looked at her. Deep in my heart I knew she was right.

"But more important, it's not *what* you're looking for, Jacob. It's *why* you're looking. You're looking because, deep inside of you, that little boy is still afraid that he's not lovable. So sometimes he pushes love away. And sometimes he tries to earn that love. But then he resents everyone he tried so hard to get to love him. He has to. Because even that little boy knows that love can't be earned. The only true love is grace. All else is a counterfeit.

"So let me answer your question, Jacob. Why weren't you lovable? The answer is something you know but haven't had the courage to believe. You see, it's possible to know things and not believe them. The true answer is this: you *were* lovable. You were a darling, bright-eyed little boy who brightened everyone's lives. Even your mother's. You were immensely lovable. You always were and you always will be. And it was that very love you had that made you so vulnerable."

She looked at me with piercing eyes. "You're still him, Jacob. You're still that sweet, bright-eyed little boy. He's still in you. And he is still loving and vulnerable. Every time I read one of your books, I can feel his sweetness rising up from the pages like groundwater. And it's not just me. So do millions of others. That's why they love you. They feel it too. And so they come to you and you fill their cups. But honey, it's time you forgot about the rest of us and filled yours."

Suddenly I began to tremble. Then tears began to well up in my eyes. Elyse slid over next to me. She put her arms around me and she too began to cry. "You darling, sweet man. I'm so sorry for your pain. I wish I could have taken it from you. But you've carried it long enough. You need to let it go."

I looked up at her. "Rachel left me. She said she loved me. Then she left me."

Elyse nodded slowly. "Of course she did. It doesn't mean she doesn't love you. It just means she fears love as much as you do. She fears abandonment as much as you do. Why else would she have come back after all these years? She's trying to answer the same question you are."

I wiped my eyes. "What do I do now?"

"Love yourself. Respect yourself. And have faith. The older I get, the more I see that things tend to work out. Not always, but usually. Just not in our time."

I looked at her gratefully and she smiled. "I brought you something." She reached into her bag and brought out a cellophane package. Brach's star-shaped chocolates. In spite of my tears, I smiled. "Oh, yes."

"And I have something else." She reached back into the bag and brought out a small polished black box. I lifted its lid. On a bed of cotton there was a glossy pin, a ceramic figurine of Batman. It flooded me with emotion. "I remember that."

"Yes. It was very special to you. I kept it at my house. You'd come over and look at it almost every day."

"The Batman pin was Nick's."

"Yes. He left it for you."

"There was a Robin pin too."

"He kept that one so you could always be the Dynamic Duo. Even when he was in Germany."

I rubbed my finger along the pin. "Such little things could bring such joy."

She looked at me. "They still do." She sighed. "So many memories."

I took her hand. "Thank you."

She slowly stood, holding on to my arm for balance. "Well, I better let you get on with your life. You've got better things to do than listen to the ramblings of an old woman."

"I don't think so," I said.

She looked into my eyes. "May I give you some advice?"

"Of course."

"When Rachel figures things out, don't punish her. She needs grace. Just like you do."

I walked her to the door. She looked out. "Oh. It's snowing again. It's always good to have snow for Christmas." She turned back and smiled. "Have a Merry Christmas, Jacob. I'm so glad you finally came home."

CHAPTER

Thirty-One

December 30, 1986

Dear Diary,

My sweet baby was born the day after Christmas. She was small, six pounds and three ounces. She's just seventeen inches long. She is so, so beautiful. Her birthday is two days after mine. Christmas will never be the same for me. They took her away from me the same day. Even my breasts are weeping for her. I can't stop crying. I don't think I'll ever see my baby again. How could I? I don't know where they took my baby. My life is shame. Why don't I fight for her? Why don't we fight for what we want?

I wonder if my baby's new parents will ever tell her about me. I wonder if this pain in my heart will ever go away.

Noel

I took a shower, shaved, and dressed, then took one last walk through the old house. One last lap. There were so many memories. Every room had memories. Far too many to take them all back with me to Coeur d'Alene. It was just as well. Many of them needed to be left here, to die with the house. But not all. There were happy memories too, times of laughter and caring. Times of love and tenderness. I just had to uncover them and give them permission to be. To coexist among the pain. Just as I had to uncover the house from my mother's hoarding.

I stood at the door of my mother's room and looked at her bed. I thought of the times I rubbed her feet or scratched her arms and face with the pencil with the toothpicks. She needed grace too. She needed to be left here too.

I took the posters down from the walls of my bedroom and was rolling them up when there was another knock. I walked out and opened the door. Standing on my porch was Rachel.

For a moment I just looked at her. Her eyes were puffy and her cheeks streaked with tears. In spite of her pain, my heart wanted to fire back at her with all the hurt she had filled it with. I remembered Elyse's words. *Grace.*

I took a deep breath. "Do you want to come in?"

Without speaking, she nodded and stepped inside. I gestured to the couch, and she sat down. I sat down across from her. She looked at me anxiously.

"Why are you here?" I asked.

"I wanted to see you."

"You rejected me. Twice."

She looked down, and I could see tears falling from her eyes. "I'm so sorry."

"You said you wanted him."

She wiped her face, then looked up. "You knew the truth."

"I'm not sure I do."

She looked at me, new pain evident on her face. Then she said, "She came."

"Who came?"

"My mother."

I let the words settle. "Is that why you're here? Because Noel told you to come see me?"

"No. I'm here because of something she said to me."

"And what was that?"

"She said, 'Don't make the same mistake I made all those years ago. I let other people write my life story.'" She looked at me vulnerably. "I wanted to see if you could love me again. Like you did. And we could change our story."

I looked at her cautiously. "Change it to what?"

She swallowed. "A romance."

"A romance?"

"Yes, like what you said. Boy meets girl, boy loses girl . . ." She hesitated. "Boy gets girl back."

I looked at her for a moment, then said, "It's a bit formulaic."

"I don't care."

"And the happily ever after?"

"There has to be a happily ever after," she said. "There's always a happily ever after when the girl finds her true love."

I looked at her for a moment, then a broad smile crossed my face. "I can write that. But only if you'll help me."

A smile crossed her face as tears fell down her cheeks. Then she jumped into my arms. "Yes. For the rest of my life, yes."

EPILOGUE

January 11, 1987

Dear Diary,

I'm preparing to go home. My parents have come to see me. They're cold. They did not see my baby. They wouldn't even speak of her. I'm afraid. I'm afraid for my little one. I'm afraid for little Jacob. I wish I could take him with me. It wouldn't be possible. I can't even bring this diary with me. It's "evidence" of a past that everyone has troubled themselves to hide. I can't bring myself to throw this diary away, so I'll just leave it in my bedroom. Maybe it will serve some purpose someday. To my little baby girl: Somehow, if you ever read this, know that I'm sorry for letting you down. To my little Jacob: Know that I will never forget you. And I will never stop loving you. I'll visit you in your dreams.

Noel

I would have liked a redux on that *USA Today* Holiday Roundup interview I did in Chicago. This time I would have much different answers. I'd tell the reporter that Christmas wasn't spent alone drinking eggnog and watching recorded games of college football.

At the last minute I flew everyone up to celebrate Christmas at my home in Coeur d'Alene. By "everyone" I mean the nine of us: Noel and Kevin; my father (yes, he got on a plane) and Gretchen; Tyson, Candace, and their son, Teonae; and Rachel and me. I had invited Elyse as well, but she had obligations with her own family.

There were a lot of stories, a lot of laughter, and a lot of tears. It was a grand celebration of *auld lang syne*.

There was also a lot of caroling as I played my piano for them. I'd had the piano tuned. It was perfect but I wasn't. It had been a while since I'd played the old songs. No one cared. Even out of tune, Christmas carols have a way of sounding sweet. One song I got right was "Greensleeves." Or the Christmas version of it, "What Child Is This?" Noel and Rachel held each other and cried.

Noel was genuinely happy. You could see it in her eyes. You could feel it in her embraces. I was glad. She deserved happiness. After I'd left her home that day, she had told her husband everything. But she did it right. It wasn't a confessional and she wasn't seeking amnesty. It was a reclamation of her authentic self. She was finally claiming her life as her own and standing in the light and power of that truth. No wonder she was filled with such joy.

✦

The next June, Rachel and I had everyone back up to Coeur d'Alene for our wedding at a beautiful resort on the lake. This time Elyse came. And Laurie, of course. All my favorite people in one place. Two months after our honeymoon in Bali, I sent Noel and Rachel off to Paris while I started on my next book. I called it *The Noel Diary*.

I sent my ladies to Paris because I thought it might be a good place for them to get to know each other better. Hemingway went there for inspiration; I figured what better place for them to start writing their own story?

That next year I even found peace with my mother. I realized that, in a twisted way, I had held on to my pain as a way to punish my mother—a woman I hadn't seen in decades. It's like they say, holding on to anger is like swallowing poison and hoping someone else will die. I was ready to let go of my pain and live. The next Mother's Day I took flowers to her grave. I knelt down and kissed her stone and thanked her for life. We chain ourselves to those we don't forgive. For the first time in my life I was truly free. I also poured a bottle of root beer on Charles's grave. He loved the stuff.

I ended up going back to Utah twice that year. Both times to cemeteries. First to see my mother's grave, then for Elyse's funeral. She suffered a stroke in October and passed away. Her family invited me to speak at her funeral. I was grateful for the honor. Nick, her nephew, was there. It was amazing to see him again. Somehow still felt like we were friends. As sad as I was at her passing, I am filled with unspeakable gratitude that she was still there when I came back home. Maybe God is in the details.

I don't have the dreams anymore. I miss them sometimes, but it seems more for nostalgia's sake than anything else. I don't need them. I have Rachel to hold me at night. She's all the love I need. And when I wake up in the morning, she's still there.

Other than in my continued production of books, my life has changed in quantum leaps. *Quantum leaps.* It's funny how often in my writing I use metaphors from physics to describe people or situations: gravity, black holes, magnetism. Perhaps, in the end, life is just a matter of physics. Life is, after all, Newton's first law of motion—the law of inertia. The law states that an object in motion stays in motion in the same direction unless acted upon by an unbalanced force.

That's the way we live our lives. We speed on, happily or not, in the same direction until we collide into something that alters our destination. Sometimes that collision hurts, sometimes it doesn't, but if we're lucky, love is that unbalanced force. Love. There is no greater force in the universe. Now if we'll only learn to stop getting out of its way.

ACKNOWLEDGMENTS

I would like to thank and acknowledge those who have journeyed alongside me with this book: Jonathan Karp, Carolyn Reidy, and the entire Simon & Schuster family. Thank you to my editor, Christine Pride, for great insight as well as remarkable patience and continual forbearance. Also, thank you to my agent, Laurie Liss, who was and is always there for me and my family. Thank you to my bestselling author daughter, Jenna Evans Welch (*Love & Gelato*) for her counsel and help with this book. It's every parent's dream to see their children rise higher than themselves, and Jenna is well on her way. I'd like to acknowledge my staff and friends, Diane Glad, Heather McVey, Barry Evans, Fran Platt, Camille Shosted, and Karen Christoffersen, for their help in sharing my books with the world.

The Noel Diary draws more from my own life than perhaps anything I've ever written. I have my own Noel. I am grateful to her and for all those who have helped to heal my emotional cuts and bruises, especially my courageous wife and friend, Keri.

Again, thank you to my readers. Without you, it's just paper and ink.

ABOUT THE AUTHOR

Richard Paul Evans is the #1 bestselling author of *The Christmas Box* and the Michael Vey series. Each of his more than thirty novels has been a *New York Times* bestseller. There are more than thirty million copies of his books in print worldwide, translated into more than twenty-four languages. He is the recipient of numerous awards, including the American Mothers Book Award, the Romantic Times Best Women's Novel of the Year Award, the German Audience Gold Award for Romance, four Religion Communicators Council Wilbur Awards, the Washington Times Humanitarian of the Century Award, and the Volunteers of America National Empathy Award. He lives in Salt Lake City, Utah, with his wife, Keri, not far from their five children and two grandchildren. You can learn more about Richard on Facebook at www.facebook.com/RPEfans or read his blog at www.richardpaulevans.com.

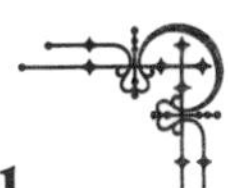

Get into the holiday spirit with all of these heartwarming stories from RICHARD PAUL EVANS!

THE NOEL COLLECTION

COMING NOVEMBER 2018!

COMING NOVEMBER 2019!

THE MISTLETOE COLLECTION

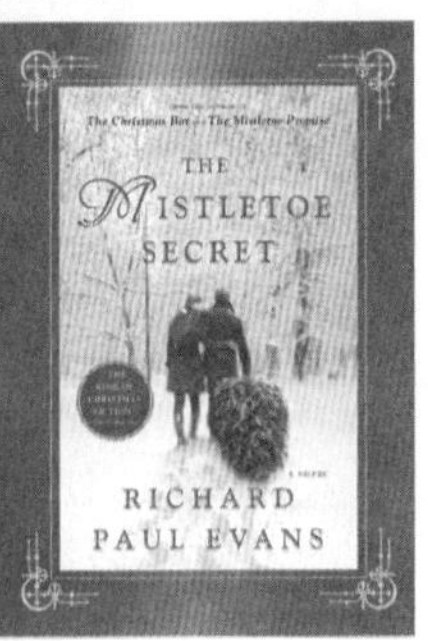

Pick up or download your copies today!

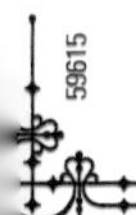
59615

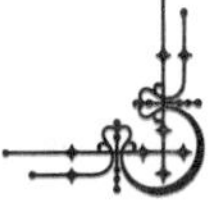